The African American Experience

Sandy Donovan

Twenty-First Century Books · Minneapolis

This book takes a broad look at African Americans. However, like all cultural groups, the African American community is extremely diverse. Each member of this community relates to his or her background and heritage in different ways, and each has had a different experience of what it means to be African American.

USA TODAY®, its logo, and associated graphics are federally registered trademarks. All rights are reserved. All USA TODAY text, graphics, and photographs are used pursuant to a license and may not be reproduced, distributed, or otherwise used without the express written consent of Gannett Co., Inc.

USA TODAY Snapshots®, graphics, and excerpts from USA TODAY articles quoted on back cover and on pages 12, 13, 26, 34, 37, 39, 43, 46, 49, 54–55, and 66–67
© copyright 2011 by USA TODAY.

Copyright © 2011 by Lerner Publishing Group, Inc.

All rights reserved. International copyright secured. No part of this book may be reproduced, stored in a retrieval system, or transmitted in any form or by any means—electronic, mechanical, photocopying, recording, or otherwise—without the prior written permission of Lerner Publishing Group, Inc., except for the inclusion of brief quotations in an acknowledged review.

Twenty-First Century Books
A division of Lerner Publishing Group, Inc.
241 First Avenue North
Minneapolis, MN 55401 U.S.A.

Website address: www.lernerbooks.com

Library of Congress Cataloging-in-Publication Data

Donovan, Sandra, 1967–
  The African American experience / by Sandy Donovan.
    p.   cm. — (USA TODAY cultural mosaic)
  Includes bibliographical references and index.
  ISBN 978–0–7613–4084–3 (lib. bdg. : alk. paper)
  1. African Americans—History--Juvenile literature. 2. African Americans—Social life and customs--Juvenile literature. I. Title.
E185.2.D66 2011
973'.0496073—dc22   2009045924

Manufactured in the United States of America
1 – DP – 7/15/10

5	**INTRODUCTION:** FROM AFRICA TO AMERICA
6	**CHAPTER 1:** LEARNING A NEW LANGUAGE
17	**CHAPTER 2:** AFRICAN AMERICANS IN THE ARTS
28	**CHAPTER 3:** ON THE PLAYING FIELD
42	**CHAPTER 4:** RELIGION
50	**CHAPTER 5:** CELEBRATING AFRICAN AMERICAN CULTURE
59	**CHAPTER 6:** FOOD

70	FAMOUS AFRICAN AMERICANS
72	EXPLORE YOUR HERITAGE
74	AFRICAN AMERICAN SNAPSHOT
75	GLOSSARY
76	SOURCE NOTE
76	SELECTED BIBLIOGRAPHY
77	FURTHER READING AND WEBSITES
78	INDEX

A U.S. Marine holds a U.S. flag at a ceremony in 2007.

USA TODAY CULTURAL MOSAIC

INTRODUCTION:
FROM AFRICA TO AMERICA

Nearly 14 percent of all U.S. residents have roots in Africa. The ancestors of most African Americans came to North America as slaves. Slave traders kidnapped men, women, and children from their homes in Africa. They sold these people to merchants. The merchants shipped Africans across the Atlantic Ocean and sold them to white Americans. The Atlantic slave trade lasted from the 1400s to the 1800s.

A debate among Americans over slavery led to the Civil War (1861–1865). After the war, African Americans became free citizens. But they continued to face racial discrimination (unfair treatment). The dominant white society limited their access to schools, jobs, and housing. African Americans led the civil rights movement (1955–1968) to gain equal rights. They won many legal rights. But discrimination against African Americans still exists.

African Americans have preserved many African traditions during their long history in the United States. They are proud of their unique and important contributions to North American society, from George Washington Carver's invention of peanut butter to Barack Obama, the first black U.S. president.

Many Africans have come voluntarily to the United States in modern times. Like other immigrants, they are looking for a better life or are fleeing war in their homeland. These African Americans have a very different experience from those whose ancestors were slaves. This book explores the cultures of all African Americans.

CHAPTER 1:
LEARNING A NEW LANGUAGE

Africa is a vast continent. Africans speak hundreds of different languages. Some recent African immigrants to the United States speak the languages of their home countries. But all African Americans speak—or are learning—English.

LOST LANGUAGE

Most of the early African Americans came to North America as slaves. Merchants in the Atlantic slave trade (between Africa and North America) stole people from central Africa's west coast. The people who lived there spoke many different languages.

Slave traders didn't want slaves to rebel. So they loaded ships with Africans who spoke different languages. This strategy ensured that the slaves on one ship could not communicate easily.

Slaves work in the cotton fields at a plantation in the southern United States in the mid- to late 1800s.

6 • THE AFRICAN AMERICAN EXPERIENCE

When slave ships reached North America, the traders sold their human cargo to landowners who needed cheap labor. Landowners had the same worries as slave traders. They did not want their slaves to work together to escape or overthrow their masters. So landowners paid more for groups of slaves who spoke different languages.

Many U.S. slaves lived on large farms in the South called plantations. Plantations grew cash crops such as cotton, sugarcane, or tobacco. Adults and children alike worked in the fields and the houses of their owners. Masters rarely let slaves speak in their home languages. Slaves had to learn English from their masters.

But parents often spoke to children in their home languages. So slave children grew up learning both English and an African language. People from different African groups used English or invented new ways to talk with one another. They created a homegrown mixture of English and African called pidgin.

The Newest African Americans

Since the 1990s, an especially large number of Africans have immigrated to the United States. During the 1990s alone, more than a half million Africans arrived. These immigrants come from many countries, including Nigeria, Ethiopia, Ghana, Sudan, and Somalia. They have fled violent conflicts or extreme poverty to start over in U.S. cities such as Washington, D.C.; Houston, Texas; and Minneapolis, Minnesota. Many African immigrants are highly educated and know English before they arrive in the United States.

Gullah

Some descendants of Africans still speak a type of pidgin called Gullah. Gullah gets most of its words from English. Its grammar and some words come from several African languages. The language probably developed in the 1700s among slaves living along the coast of South Carolina, Georgia, and northeastern Florida. Some Gullah speakers lived on tiny sea islands. Since the island communities have always been somewhat isolated, the Gullah language survived there. About 250,000 African Americans still speak it.

Slave English was not standard English. Slaves never went to school, so they didn't learn standard grammar. Masters forbade slaves to learn how to read or write. However, many enslaved Africans came from cultures that valued oral (spoken) literature. Slave elders drew on this tradition as they taught their children new stories in a new world.

FROM SLAVE TO FREE

From the 1600s to the 1800s, merchants shipped more than half a million African slaves to North America. Some free African Americans lived in the United States too. Some had come by choice. Others had escaped slavery, bought their freedom, or been freed by their owners. In the 1800s, many U.S. states abolished (outlawed) slavery. Slaves in those states became free. But most free African Americans still couldn't go to school.

After the Civil War, slavery became illegal in all states. Many former slaves moved from plantations to cities looking for jobs. And many African Americans left the South to seek opportunity in the North and the West.

But the dominant white society in most cities did not accept African Americans as equals. So they took low-paying jobs as laborers. Most African Americans could afford to live only in run-down neighborhoods. Their children had little opportunity to attend school. Christian churches were important places of cultural expression for black people. The speaking style of many preachers drew on the strong oral traditions of Africa and the slave era.

Through the 1900s, many African Americans lived in tightly knit communities. An African American dialect (variety of English) with its own grammar and vocabulary flourished in black neighborhoods. Most people called this dialect black English. In the 1970s, some scholars named it Ebonics. This word combines *ebony* (a black wood from Africa) and *phonics* (the science of sound).

By the 2000s, some Americans were debating: Is Ebonics a valuable expression of African American culture and a rich contribution to the larger culture, or is it a "wrong" way of speaking English? Many African Americans who grew up speaking Ebonics choose to speak standard English to succeed in mainstream society. Many feel that they are bilingual (able to speak two languages).

DEVELOPING PRIDE THROUGH LITERATURE

Throughout the nineteenth and into the twentieth centuries, African Americans worked to overcome the impact of slavery. For much of that time, anyone with dark skin had trouble getting formal education, decent housing, and good-paying jobs.

A strong tradition of storytelling helped people during these times. African Americans combined memories and customs from their homelands with experiences and wisdom gained in the United States to create a rich tapestry of folktales. For example, black slaves wove stories in which animals took on the traits of various plantation people. The rabbit, often called Br'er (Brother) Rabbit, was a favorite of African American storytellers. Rabbit was small and seemingly helpless. But he was smart and tricky, and he used his skills to outwit bigger and stronger animals. Sometimes he got in trouble, which made him seem human. Many slaves saw themselves in Br'er Rabbit.

African Americans recognized that the printed word was a powerful weapon against discrimination. They could also use it to tell their unique story. So against difficult odds, many African Americans learned to read and write English. In the late 1800s and early 1900s, more and more African Americans attended school. Most black children went to school for only a few years. But some completed high school. A smaller number went on to college.

One of the most highly educated African Americans of this period was William Edward Burghardt (W. E. B.) DuBois. DuBois was born in Massachusetts in 1868. He was poor, and he believed he could improve his family's life

W. E. B. DuBois was an important thinker and writer. He helped found the National Association for the Advancement of Colored People (NAACP) in the early 1900s.

through education. In 1895 he became the first African American to earn a PhD—the highest degree—from Harvard University in Massachusetts.

DuBois studied and wrote about history, politics, education, and discrimination. He was a journalist, a book author, and a publisher. In some of his early books, he described African American contributions to U.S. history. In 1909 DuBois helped start the National Association for the Advancement of Colored People (NAACP). This group works to achieve equal rights for African Americans.

In 1910 DuBois became the editor of NAACP's magazine, the *Crisis*. Around this time, an African American arts scene sprang up in New York City's Harlem neighborhood. DuBois published many of Harlem's writers in the *Crisis*. This helped their careers grow.

Among the writers DuBois launched were Langston Hughes and Zora Neale Hurston. Hughes published more than fifty books of poetry, fiction, nonfiction, drama, and children's literature in his lifetime (1902–1967). Hurston published four novels and more than fifty short stories, plays, and essays. Her most famous work, *Their Eyes Were Watching God*, was published in 1937.

By the 1940s and 1950s, more African American authors were publishing books. Several wrote about the experience of being black in the United States. In 1940 Richard Wright published *Native Son*. This novel tells the story of a black man's struggles with poverty, crime, and racism in Chicago, Illinois. It became one of the first best-selling books by an African American author. In 1953 Ralph Ellison won the National Book Award for his novel *Invisible Man*. In this book, an unnamed black narrator tells about the experience of being invisible to white society.

Martin Luther King Jr. *(center)* speaks at a church service in Harlem, New York, in March 1968. King's stirring speeches helped further equal rights for African Americans.

By the 1960s, many African Americans were working together to fight for equal rights. Martin Luther King Jr. was the most famous leader in the civil rights movement. He often used speeches and essays to advance his goals. As a preacher himself, he based his speaking and writing on the style of African American preachers. They drew on African American oral traditions.

King's "Letter from Birmingham Jail" is a famous example of his writing. He wrote this essay in April 1963, while in prison in Alabama for organizing civil rights protests. King delivered his famous "I have a dream" speech in August 1963 from the steps of the Lincoln Memorial in Washington, D.C.

USA TODAY Snapshots®

When Americans expected a black president

Asked in 2001 when the USA would have its first black president, percentage of adults saying:

- Within 10 years **36%**
- Within 25 years **43%**
- After 100 years **2%**
- Never **8%**
- No opinion **2%**
- Within 100 years **9%**

Photo by Eric Draper, White House, via Reuters
Source: USA TODAY/CNN/Gallup Poll of 1,055 adults, Jan. 15-16, 2001

By Anne Carey and Keith Simmons, USA TODAY, 2009

12 · THE AFRICAN AMERICAN EXPERIENCE

November 8, 2008

From the Pages of USA TODAY

Many see dream coming true

Forty-five years ago, Fae Robinson stood in a vast crowd in Washington and heard Martin Luther King Jr.'s "I have a dream" speech. On Jan. 20, she'll be back in Washington for Barack Obama's inauguration, which she considers the fulfillment of King's dream—and her own.

On that day in August 1963, King said, "I have a dream that one day this nation will rise up and live out the true meaning of its creed: 'We hold these truths to be self-evident, that all men are created equal.' . . . I have a dream that my four little children will one day live in a nation where they will not be judged by the color of their skin but by the content of their character."

Robinson had come to Washington on a bus with other students from what's now called Cheyney University of Pennsylvania, the oldest of the USA's historically black colleges. As she listened to King, she thought, "Yes, I know what you mean. Yes, I have the same dream. Yes, maybe one day it will come true," she says. "I didn't really think I would be alive to see it, but Obama is the result of that dream."

Robinson is among thousands of people, many of them black, who don't have tickets to the swearing-in or other inaugural events but feel compelled to

Afi Johnson-Parris is overcome with emotion at Barack Obama's inauguration as president on January 20, 2009.

be in the capital when the nation's first black president takes office.

When Obama defeated John McCain on Nov. 4, it didn't take long for Robinson, who is the pastor of Albright-Bethune United Methodist Church in State College, Pa., to decide to make the four-hour trip to Washington again. "I told everybody, 'I'm going,'" she says. "I don't have to have a ticket. I just want to be somewhere close. I have to be there. Just to be there is going to be overwhelming."

She will join members of her congregation on a bus for the trip.

—*Judy Keen*

THRIVING LITERARY SCENE

Starting in the 1970s, the African American literary scene exploded. More black authors than ever were being published. And more readers of all races bought works by African Americans.

In 1970 Toni Morrison published her first novel, *The Bluest Eye*. This book follows a year in the life of a troubled black girl who wishes she were white, with blue eyes. Alex Haley topped the best-seller list with his 1976 novel *Roots: The Saga of an American Family*. Alice Walker won a Pulitzer Prize for her 1982 novel *The Color Purple*. It explores the lives of two sisters during the 1930s. A few years later, Morrison won a Pulitzer for her 1987 novel *Beloved*. In this story, Morrison examines the wrenching legacy of slavery.

From the late 1980s through the early 2000s, several African American writers were regulars on best-seller lists. For example, Terry McMillan published six popular novels. Eric Jerome Dickey published more than twenty.

Author Alice Walker wrote *The Color Purple*. She won the Pulitzer Prize for this book in 1983.

Ebony

The monthly magazine *Ebony* was the first major U.S. magazine to focus on African American people, issues, and interests. A Chicago publisher named John H. Johnson started it in 1945. Johnson modeled his magazine on the most popular glossy magazine of the day, *Life* magazine. Like *Life*, *Ebony* features large photo spreads. *Ebony* reaches almost two million readers per month. Its stories often focus on achievements of African American entertainers, athletes, and politicians.

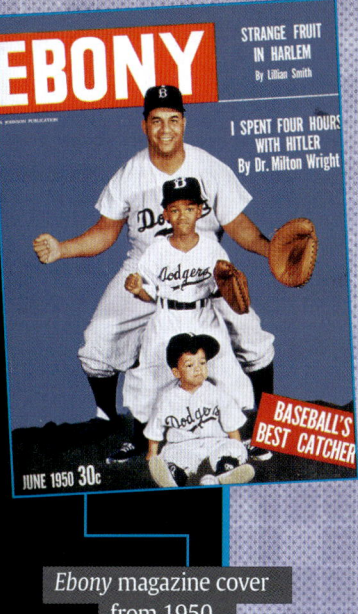

Ebony magazine cover from 1950

Omar Tyree has published sixteen books that have sold nearly two million copies. President Barack Obama wrote the critically acclaimed autobiography *Dreams from My Father* and a best seller, *The Audacity of Hope*.

Several African American poets have also achieved huge success. Gwendolyn Brooks and Rita Dove each won a Pulitzer Prize for poetry. Maya Angelou read her poem "On the Pulse of Morning" at President Bill Clinton's inauguration in 1993. And Elizabeth Alexander read her poem "Praise Song for the Day" at the 2009 inauguration of President Obama.

The gospel choir from Virginia State University performs at a competition in New York.

USA TODAY CULTURAL MOSAIC

CHAPTER 2:
AFRICAN AMERICANS IN THE ARTS

African Americans have contributed to almost every type of American art. Some of the country's best-known musicians, painters, actors, and filmmakers have African roots. The history of African Americans in the arts reflects their unique journey.

FROM SPIRITUALS TO JAZZ

Music has played a key role in African American life. In Africa, music was a common form of celebration, worship, and communication. When Africans came as slaves to North America, they held onto their musical traditions. In many cases, music was one of their only links to the past.

Spirituals were an early musical tradition among Africans in the United States. Slaves gathered on plantations to sing songs such as "This Little Light of Mine" and "Swing Low, Sweet Chariot." Most spirituals were Christian praise songs. (Christians follow the teachings of Jesus Christ.) Few Africans were Christian, but U.S. masters taught their slaves Christianity. Some slaves saw their lives reflected in Bible stories. For example, the story of Moses leading the Hebrews (ancestors of modern Jews) out of slavery in Egypt gave African Americans hope. They sang of this story in spirituals such as "Go Down, Moses." Even after the Civil War, African Americans continued to long for a "promised land" of liberty and justice. Spirituals therefore remained popular among African Americans.

Blues music has roots in spirituals and work songs from slavery times. Around 1900 many people who had been slaves were working as sharecroppers across the South. These tenant farmers lived and worked on other people's land. They had to give much of their crop harvests to the landowners as rent. Although sharecroppers were free Americans, they did backbreaking work for long hours and little money. Their lives were extremely difficult.

To endure hardship, sharecroppers sang work songs similar to spirituals. Some were call-and-response songs. In a call-and-response song, one person sings a line and others echo it. Meanwhile, juke joints sprang up across the South. These were informal gathering spots offering music, dancing, gambling, and drinking. At juke joints, musicians performed their own versions of work songs with acoustic guitars, pianos, and harmonicas. The lyrics described sharecroppers' suffering, often using a call-and-response style. This music became known as the blues. The term *blues* means "sadness." The name of this music also comes from its use of "blue notes," or flat tones (in Western music, notes lowered by a half step).

Juke

The term *juke* comes from the Gullah word *juk,* meaning "rowdy and wicked." The word *jukebox* describes a coin-operated cabinet record player found in many juke joints.

Musician W. C. Handy is often called the Father of the Blues.

In 1909 the African American musician W. C. Handy published sheet music for a song called "Memphis Blues." This widely sold song introduced mainstream U.S. society to the blues. Handy went on to become a pioneering blues musician and bandleader. By the 1940s, blues music had grown popular throughout the South. Poor blacks and whites alike related to the difficulties described in blues songs.

By the mid-1900s, many African Americans had moved to northern cities to find factory work. They developed music to reflect their urban lifestyle. Blues musicians such as Muddy Waters traded acoustic guitars for electric guitars. They also added drums and stand-up bass or bass guitar. The electric blues sound got people onto dance floors in cities across the United States. It also paved the way for the birth of rock 'n' roll.

Meanwhile, jazz music was also gaining many fans. Jazz draws on blues as well as ragtime. Ragtime is dance music with a ragged, or syncopated, rhythm. It was popular between the 1890s and 1920s. Jazz blended blue notes with ragtime's ragged rhythms to create a unique sound. It also drew on big-band orchestral music.

Black artists such as trumpeter Louis Armstrong and pianist Jelly Roll Morton were jazz pioneers. African American singers Lena Horne and Billie Holiday were successful with both black and white audiences in the 1930s and 1940s. Bandleaders Count Basie and Duke Ellington toured the United States and Europe. African Americans such as saxophonist Charlie Parker, pianist Thelonius Monk, and singer Ella Fitzgerald all left their own unique stamp on jazz.

FROM ROCK 'N' ROLL TO HIP-HOP

In the 1950s, African Americans contributed to the birth of more American music. Both rock 'n' roll and soul music took off in that decade.

Chuck Berry, a black guitar player from Saint Louis, Missouri, became known as the King of Rock 'n' Roll. Chuck Berry songs such as "Sweet Little Sixteen" and "Johnny B. Goode" were smash hits with white teens across the United States in the late 1950s. When white musicians, such as Elvis Presley, took up this African American style, they rose in the charts too.

Another African American, Ray Charles, was one of the most successful U.S. musicians ever. Charles introduced the world to soul music. Soul music mixes blues and black gospel music. In 1959 Charles's song "What'd I Say" earned him a huge following among both blacks and whites.

Many black musicians rose to fame as soul artists in the 1960s. Some stayed popular through the following decades as stars of funk, disco, and hip-hop.

For instance, the soul star James Brown shot to fame in the 1960s with songs such as "Ain't That a Groove." A decade later, he had a string of funk and disco hits, such as "Hot Pants." In 1980 Brown

Ray Charles was inducted into the Rock and Roll Hall of Fame in 1986. Here he performs at a Rock and Roll Hall of Fame concert in New York in 2000.

Aretha Franklin is often called the Queen of Soul. She performed at the inauguration of President Barack Obama in 2009.

was a hit in the movie *The Blues Brothers*.

Motown Records, a Detroit company founded by Berry Gordy in 1959, played an important role in ending popular music's racial divide in the 1960s and 1970s. Gordy had a knack for turning African American street singers and unknown bands into mainstream music stars. Motown launched the careers of such superstars as Diana Ross, Aretha Franklin, and Michael Jackson.

Throughout the 1960s, Diana Ross and the Supremes, a female soul trio, were wildly popular around the world. Their fame and commercial success opened a door to mainstream pop music for later African American artists.

Another enduring soul star is Aretha Franklin. Franklin wowed Americans during the 1960s with dynamic songs like "Respect." In 1987, she became the first woman to be inducted into the Rock and Roll Hall of Fame. She sang for President Obama's inauguration in 2009. Franklin has won numerous awards, including a Grammy Lifetime Achievement Award.

In the late 1960s, a group of young African American brothers called the Jackson 5 had a string of number one hits. The group changed its name to the Jacksons and continued to top the charts throughout the 1970s. In 1979 brother Michael Jackson released his first solo album. After releasing his wildly popular album *Thriller* in 1982, he became one of the world's most famous artists. His popularity smashed racial barriers in pop music. Jackson continued recording, touring, and winning awards until his sudden death in June 2009. *Thriller* remains the best-selling album ever.

Some of the country's most popular sounds, such as rap and hip-hop, grew out of African musical traditions and African American neighborhoods. Rap features rhyming lyrics spoken to a rhythmic beat, much like the style of West African storytellers called griots. In modern times, the lyrics reflect life in poor, black neighborhoods. Some Americans criticize the violence in rap lyrics. Others praise rap for taking an honest look at the experience of poor black youth.

Hip-hop music features rap lyrics over dance music, usually with a strong drumbeat. Hip-hop came out of New York in the 1970s, when graffiti writing exploded as a related art form. Hip-hop stars such as Jay-Z, Beyoncé, and Kanye West have many fans all over the world.

STAGE AND SCREEN

African Americans have played a role in American theater for two centuries. In the early 1800s, a type of theater called minstrel grew popular. Minstrel shows featured African Americans as the main characters. However, these shows portrayed their characters as stupid, lazy, and superstitious. Also, white actors in blackface (dark facial makeup) played all the roles. After the Civil War, blacks began performing in minstrel shows.

By the early 1900s, African Americans had staged several all-black musicals. But black theater didn't earn much notice until the Harlem Renaissance of the 1920s and 1930s. During that period, in 1924, singer and dancer Florence Mills became the first black woman to headline a Broadway musical show.

Chamillionaire

The Grammy-winning rapper and hip-hop artist Chamillionaire *(right)* is an example of the diversity of African American experience. His father is an immigrant from Nigeria and his mother is an African American from an established U.S. family. He was born in Washington, D.C., and moved to Houston, Texas, when he was four years old.

Chamillionaire's given name is Hakeem Seriki. For the name Chamillionaire, he mixed the words *chameleon* and *millionaire*. A chameleon is a lizard that changes colors to blend into its surroundings. Chamillionaire says that he is always open to change.

Chamillionaire held many jobs before he entered the music business. He stocked trucks. He drove blood and urine samples to medical labs. He passed out flyers promoting hip-hop clubs.

Chamillionaire began rapping in 1998 and made his first album in 2002. He became known around Houston. In 2005 he made his first big solo album, *The Sound of Revenge*. The album reached number ten on the Billboard music charts, and his single "Ridin'" reached number one on the singles charts. "Ridin'" was a statement about the police practice of racial profiling—treating black people unfairly and differently from white people. The song earned Chamillionaire a Grammy Award in 2007.

Since then Chamillionaire has continued to record rap songs with strong messages. For example, his song "Hip-Hop Police" explores how society sometimes blames rap music for crime.

(Broadway, a street in New York City, is the most influential U.S. theater district.) Fifteen years later, Ethel Waters became the first black woman to star in a dramatic play on Broadway. Paul Robeson became famous for a powerful performance on Broadway in 1943, playing the lead role in Shakespeare's play *Othello*.

In addition to acting, Paul Robeson (above in *Othello*) was a lawyer and civil rights activist.

Many plays in the 1940s and 1950s, such as Lorraine Hansberry's 1959 Broadway play *A Raisin in the Sun*, explored the ongoing effects of racism in the United States. In the 1960s, playwrights such as Amiri Baraka created works that directly attacked racism. In 1975 the award-winning Broadway musical *The Wiz* retold L. Frank Baum's story *The Wonderful Wizard of Oz* in the context of African American culture.

By the end of the century, theater had become more integrated (racially diverse). In the early 2000s, black performers and playwrights are common on and off Broadway.

African American actors have contributed to the growth of U.S. cinema as well. The earliest film depictions of African Americans were insulting and stereotypical (oversimplified). For example, the first movie with an all-black cast was *The Wooing and Wedding of a Coon* (1905). The word *coon* was an offensive name for African Americans. The movie conveyed African Americans as lazy and stupid. Decades passed before smart black characters appeared in films for white audiences. In 1936 the movie *Show Boat* handled racial topics in a way that was enlightened for its time. Paul Robeson brought dignity to the character Joe. Hattie McDaniel, also in *Show Boat*, became the first black actor to win an Academy Award. She won for her portrayal of the slave Mammy in *Gone with the Wind* (1939).

Since his first feature film in 1985, the director, producer, and writer Spike Lee has been a major force in U.S. movies. His screenplay for *Do the Right Thing* was nominated for an Academy Award in 1989. Lee's biopic *Malcolm X* (1992) sparked new interest in the African American civil rights figure.

Besides being a powerhouse in television, Oprah Winfrey is also a movie producer and actor. She played a key role in the movie *The Color Purple* (1985), produced and starred in *Beloved* (1998), and coproduced *Precious* (2009).

Some of modern Hollywood's leading actors and actresses are African American. In 2002 Halle Berry and Denzel Washington became the first black actress and actor to win an Academy Award for lead roles. For their work in the 2009 film *Precious: Based on the Novel 'Push' by Sapphire*, Gabourey Sidibe received a 2010 Academy Award nomination for Best Actress, and Mo'Nique won the Academy Award for Best Supporting Actress. Will Smith is one of Hollywood's highest-paid actors. African American comedians, such as Whoopi Goldberg, Bill Cosby, Chris Rock, Tyler Perry, and Eddie Murphy, have many fans among Americans of all ethnic backgrounds.

Denzel Washington and Halle Berry won Academy Awards in 2002 for their roles in *Training Day* (Washington) and *Monster's Ball* (Berry).

March 8, 2010

From the Pages of USA TODAY
A night of emotion, a night of thanks

The best seat at the Oscars is backstage. USA TODAY's Anthony Breznican was in the wings of the Kodak Theatre Sunday night, capturing off-the-cuff moments that followed the staged events.

One of the most emotional moments backstage came after screenwriter Geoffrey Fletcher won for his adapted screenplay to *Precious: Based on the Novel 'Push' by Saphire* and Mo'Nique won supporting actress for playing the film's malevolent mother.

Known for her brassy and blunt comedy, Mo'Nique humbled the audience by thanking the academy for showing that the awards "can be about the performance, not the politics."

And she thanked Hattie McDaniel, the first African American to win an Oscar for playing Mammy in 1939's *Gone With the Wind.* "I want to thank Miss Hattie McDaniel for enduring all that she had to so I would not have to," the actress said.

Mo'Nique had been criticized by some Oscar pundits for not aggressively campaigning throughout awards season. It didn't seem to hurt her; she won almost every major prize before also taking home the academy award.

As she walked off stage, there was no sign of sassiness or ego. She grabbed hold of stage manager Valdez Flagg and said softly, "Can you just hold me?" And the two hugged in silence for a long time.

Waiting just behind her in the shadows was Fletcher, his Oscar demurely held at his side. Onstage, Fletcher said, "This is for everybody who works on a dream every day. Precious boys and girls everywhere."

One of the ABC pages came by and said, "Does anyone know where Geoffrey Fletcher is?" while looking directly at him. "Do you have eyes on Geoffrey Fletcher?"

Fletcher raised his Oscar into view and with a stunned look asked, "Me? Do you mean me?" But before he would let the page take him to the pressroom in the hotel next door, he wanted his moment with Mo'Nique. Another hug—this one much longer—ensued. But it wasn't silent.

"Oh, baby! Oh, baby," Mo'Nique repeated again and again, as they clutched their Oscars at the other's back. "Look what we did!"

As they pulled apart, they raised their Oscars and clinked their heads like champagne glasses. "To you," Mo'Nique said. "To you, my baby.'"

—*Anthony Breznican*

PAINTING, SCULPTURE, AND PHOTOGRAPHY

African American artists have brought riches to the visual arts in the United States. In the days of slavery, African Americans had limited resources. But craftspeople and folk artists kept alive African traditions and created new ones. These included basket weaving, pottery, metalworking, and wood carving. Women sewed designs and told stories with their handmade quilts.

Some Western-style fine artists emerged too. Joshua Johnson was one of the first professional African American artists. His white father purchased him out of slavery in the late 1700s. He went on to become a well-known portrait painter in Baltimore, Maryland.

Nearly one hundred years later, Edmonia Lewis was a famous sculptor. Lewis was born a free African American in the northern United States. She was one of the few women—black or white—to attend college in the 1800s.

In the 1900s and early 2000s, many African Americans made names for themselves as visual artists. William H. Johnson, Jacob Lawrence, and Hughie Lee-Smith were all painters. Gordon Parks and Earlie Hudnall Jr. were photographers. Betye Saar and Renee Stout were famous mixed-media artists. Modern artist Kara Walker cuts black paper into room-sized silhouettes. In 2007 *Time* magazine named Walker one of one hundred most influential artists in the world.

This painting by Hughie Lee-Smith is titled *The Stranger* and dates from 1957–1958. It is at the Smithsonian American Art Museum in Washington, D.C.

CHAPTER 3:
ON THE PLAYING FIELD

Watch any professional major-league sport, and you'll see African Americans in the game. In fact, you might see more African Americans than Americans of other races. About 14 percent of all Americans have African roots. But 65 percent of National Football League (NFL) players are black. And 82 percent of National Basketball Association (NBA) players are black. African Americans are also prominent in baseball, tennis, boxing, track and field, and many other sports.

Los Angeles Lakers player Kobe Bryant goes up for a shot in the Lakers playoff game against the Orlando Magic in 2009.

SEGREGATED SPORTS

It wasn't always this way. Until the 1940s, sports were mostly segregated. Black athletes were forbidden to compete with white Americans in sports. Sports were important to African Americans. So they found ways to participate in separate leagues.

Some black athletes defied segregation. For example, cyclist Marshall Taylor took on discrimination and ignored physical and verbal attacks as he raced in the 1890s and early 1900s. After setting numerous world records, he won the world 1-mile (1.6-kilometer) track cycling championship in 1899.

Some African Americans formed black sports clubs. The first of these was the Smart Set Club. It opened in 1905 in New York City. The club had both male and female teams. Basketball and track were the club's most popular sports.

Meanwhile, black baseball teams were growing popular across the country. African Americans had played baseball throughout the 1800s—often alongside white players. But by the early 1900s, no major-league teams had black baseball players. Many all-black teams sprang up. By the 1920s, the owners of those teams began to form black baseball leagues. The Negro National League, the Negro Southern League, and the Eastern Colored League were successful from the 1920s until the late 1940s, when major-league teams began drafting black baseball players.

African American women athletes excelled in the early 1900s too. In 1910 the New York Girls became the first independent all-black female basketball team. Black women found particular success in running track. In 1927 the Tuskegee Institute, a college in Alabama for African Americans, began the Tuskegee Relays. These were mostly competitions for men, but they featured two events for women. The Relays gave Tuskegee's female students a goal to reach for. The school soon hosted many of the fastest women runners in the country. In 1932 the track stars Louise Stokes and Tydia Pickett became the first African American women to compete in the Olympic Games.

Jackie Robinson was the first African American to play for a Major League Baseball team. Here he leaps to make a catch in 1947.

BREAKING THE COLOR BARRIER

In the next decades, African Americans began breaking color barriers not only at the Olympics but also in major-league sports. In late 1945, the Brooklyn Dodgers baseball team drafted Jackie Robinson. He spent the 1946 season with the team's minor-league partner, the Montreal Royals. On April 15, 1947, in his first game with the Dodgers, he became the first African American to play in Major League Baseball.

Soon the walls dividing black and white players in other sports came down too. The Los Angeles Rams became the first team to break the NFL color barrier. In 1946 the Rams drafted two African American players, Woody Strode and Kenny Washington.

In 1950 the NBA gained its first black player when the Boston Celtics drafted Chuck Cooper. Over the next ten years, many African American stars joined professional basketball teams. These included Bill Russell, Wilt Chamberlain, Oscar Robertson, and Elgin Baylor.

30 · THE AFRICAN AMERICAN EXPERIENCE

ACTIVIST ATHLETES

By the 1960s, many pro sports teams had African American players. But still it was hard for many African Americans to find good jobs, housing, and education.

During the 1960s, many people joined the civil rights movement to demand fair treatment for black Americans. Martin Luther King Jr.'s style of peaceful protest was popular among civil rights workers. Some African American athletes adopted this protest style too. They were called activist athletes.

One of the earliest activist athletes was boxing champ Muhammad Ali. In 1960 he was going by his given name, Cassius Clay. Clay won a gold medal in the light heavyweight boxing division at the Olympic Games in Rome, Italy. But when he returned to the United States, he continued to experience discrimination. One night, after being turned away from a restaurant in his hometown of Louisville, Kentucky, Clay became angry. He flung his gold medal into the Ohio River as a protest that night, he said later. Some people say this story isn't true.

Many Americans think Muhammad Ali is the greatest boxer in history. He is shown here in 1960, when he was still known as Cassius Clay.

Nonetheless, it is true that Clay soon became an activist athlete.

In 1964 Clay won the professional heavyweight boxing title. He soon changed his name. He said the name Cassius Clay was a slave name. He became a Muslim (follower of the religion of Islam) and took the name Muhammad Ali. In 1967 the U.S. Army drafted him to serve in the Vietnam War (1957–1975). He refused to serve, saying his religion forbade warfare. The courts convicted him of a felony (serious crime). Boxing officials stripped his heavyweight title and denied him the right to box professionally.

Three years later, the Supreme Court reversed Ali's conviction. He could fight again. He soon regained the heavyweight title. Many called him the greatest boxer in history. In 1999 *Sports Illustrated* magazine named him Sports Personality of the Century.

Ali was not the only African American activist athlete. Many black athletes used their fame to help other black Americans. At the 1968 Olympic Games in Mexico City, Mexico, two sprinters named John Carlos and Tommie Smith won medals in the 200-meter race. At the medal ceremony, they bowed their heads and raised their black-gloved fists. Smith and Carlos made this well-known protest gesture to support equal rights for blacks in the United States. One wore a black scarf as a symbol of black pride. They both wore black socks and no shoes. This symbolized the poverty of many African Americans.

The protest was peaceful, and it had a strong impact. The International Olympic Committee expelled (kicked out) Smith and Carlos from the Olympics. Both runners later received hate mail and death threats. Their actions made their lives difficult for many years. But three decades later, the U.S. sports community recognized them for their courage.

THE AFRICAN AMERICAN EXPERIENCE

BREAKING RECORDS AND BATTLING RACISM

By the 1970s, most pro sports teams had black members. Many African Americans were setting records in their sports. But that didn't mean discrimination had ended.

In the early 1970s, baseball player Hank Aaron was chasing the lifetime home run record set by Babe Ruth in 1935. Across the United States, black and white fans cheered Aaron. But some whites were angry. They sent Aaron letters calling him names, threatening his life, and telling him he wasn't good enough to beat Ruth's record because he was black.

The angry letters made Aaron more determined. And many Americans spoke out against the racism. Even Ruth's widow supported Aaron. On April 8, 1974, Aaron did break the record.

Aaron kept the home run record until 2007, when Barry Bonds broke it. After Aaron retired from baseball, he was voted into the Baseball Hall of Fame. Major League Baseball named an award after him. Every year the Hank Aaron Award goes to the best hitters in each league.

Baseball great Hank Aaron poses near a statue of his likeness in Atlanta, Georgia, in 1999.

In tennis, champion Arthur Ashe is the only African American player ever to win the men's singles title at three Grand Slam events. (Grand Slam tennis competitions include the U.S. Open, the Australian Open, the French Open, and Wimbledon.) Ashe won the U.S. Open in 1968. He won the Australian Open in 1970. And he beat Jimmy Connors to win Wimbledon in 1975.

USA TODAY Snapshots®

Black History Month

Black athletes honored by halls

Today marks the start of Black History Month. Years that the first black athletes were inducted into various sports' halls of fame:

Baseball Hall of Fame **Jackie Robinson**	1962
Pro Football Hall of Fame **Emlen Tunnell**	1967
International Tennis Hall of Fame **Althea Gibson**	1971
Naismith Memorial Basketball Hall of Fame **Robert J. Douglas**	1972
Hockey Hall of Fame **Grant Fuhr**	2003
World Golf Hall of Fame **Charlie Sifford**	2004

Source: USA TODAY research
By Ellen J. Horrow and Sam Ward, USA TODAY, 2007

Ashe's 1975 win was a great moment in sports history. Many Americans were proud. But that same year, Ashe experienced vicious racism on the tennis court. He was playing against Romanian Ilie Nastase. Nastase insulted Ashe. He said he didn't want to play against a black person. Ashe tried to ignore him. He was winning the game. But finally, he walked off the court. He said, "I've had enough. I'm at

Young Champ

When Arthur Ashe was seventeen years old, he appeared in *Sports Illustrated* as the first African American to ever win the National Junior Indoor Tennis title. Ashe is shown here after winning the Wimbledon men's singles tennis championship in London, England, in 1975.

34 · THE AFRICAN AMERICAN EXPERIENCE

the point where I'm afraid I'll lose control." The game officials told him he would lose the game if he walked away. Ashe said, "I don't care. I'd rather lose that than my self-respect." In the end, the officials decided that they could not give the win to Nastase. They did not want to support his actions. So they declared Ashe the winner.

Ashe played pro tennis for four more years. After he retired, he devoted his life to working for civil rights. He died in 1993 from AIDS. Many Americans admire his work in tennis and his work for civil rights and the fight against AIDS. The tennis stadium in Flushing, New York, where the modern U.S. Open takes place, is named Arthur Ashe Stadium.

AFRICAN AMERICAN WOMEN IN SPORTS

Some of the greatest African American athletes have been women. They have excelled in track and field, tennis, and a host of other sports.

Sprinter Wilma Rudolph was the star of the 1960 Olympics. She became the first U.S. woman of any race to win three gold medals at one

Sprinter Wilma Rudolph holds the three gold medals she won in the 100 meters, 200 meters, and 4 x 100-meter relay at the 1960 Olympics.

ON THE PLAYING FIELD • 35

Sisters Venus *(left)* and Serena Williams *(right)* celebrate after winning the doubles final at the Australian Open tennis tournament in 2010.

Olympics. Florence Griffith Joyner, also known as Flo-Jo, repeated Rudolph's triple win at the 1988 Olympics.

African American women have broken barriers in tennis too. Althea Gibson became the first black American to win a Grand Slam tennis tournament at the French Open in 1956. In 1957 and 1958, Gibson won both the women's singles and doubles titles at Wimbledon. In 2000 and 2001, Venus Williams repeated Gibson's achievement. Venus's sister Serena has won more than a dozen Grand Slam events.

36 · THE AFRICAN AMERICAN EXPERIENCE

In 1996 the Women's National Basketball Association (WNBA) formed. During the league's first few years, several African American players became stars. These included Lisa Leslie, Cynthia Cooper, Tina Thompson, and Sheryl Swoopes. In 2000 the Houston Comets became the first professional women's sports team invited to the White House Rose Garden.

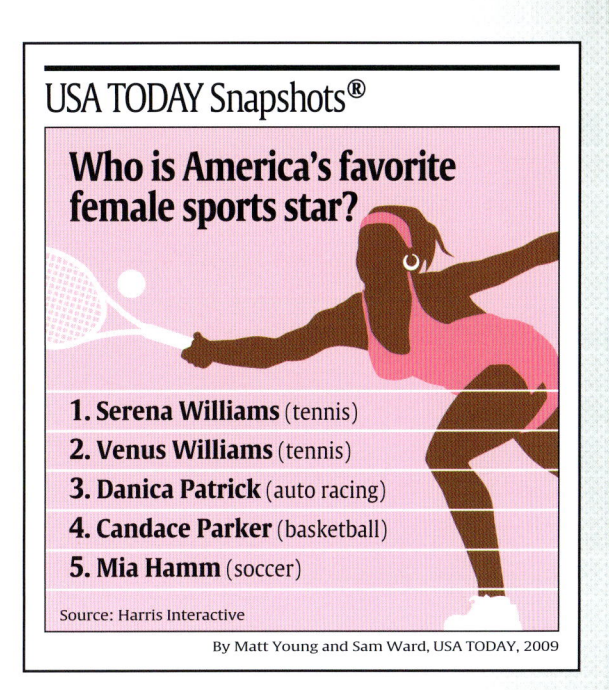

USA TODAY Snapshots®

Who is America's favorite female sports star?

1. **Serena Williams** (tennis)
2. **Venus Williams** (tennis)
3. **Danica Patrick** (auto racing)
4. **Candace Parker** (basketball)
5. **Mia Hamm** (soccer)

Source: Harris Interactive

By Matt Young and Sam Ward, USA TODAY, 2009

WNBA basketball players *(left to right)* Tina Thompson, Cynthia Cooper, Adrian Williams, and Lisa Leslie pose for a photo before the All-Star game in 2003.

RECENT SPORTS STARS

Many top sports stars of the 1990s and 2000s have been African American. Men's basketball has particularly high numbers of black superstars. Players such as Michael Jordan, Magic Johnson, Shaquille O'Neal, and Kobe Bryant have dominated the NBA.

In football, African Americans are playing in a wider variety of positions than they used to. In the 1980s, most black pro football players were defensive backs or running backs. Quarterbacks, coaches, and managers were mostly whites.

In 1988 Doug Williams became the first black quarterback to win a Super Bowl, and Johnny Grier was the NFL's first black referee. In 1989 Art Shell became the league's first African American head coach. In 2002 Ozzie Newsome was the first black general manager. In 2006 Warren Moon became the first African American quarterback inducted into the Pro Football Hall of Fame. In 2007 Tony Dungy was the first African American coach to win a Super Bowl.

Warren Moon was a quarterback for many NFL teams.

April 13, 2007

From the Pages of USA TODAY

60 years after Robinson, is his legacy fading away?

On Sunday, when more than 200 Major League Baseball [MLB] players wear No. 42 jerseys to honor the 60th anniversary of Jackie Robinson breaking the color barrier in the national pastime, it will be a reminder of past promises and a troubling present.

The commemoration of Robinson's historic debut will recall an elaborate ceremony 10 years ago, when MLB retired Robinson's number across the majors and Commissioner Bud Selig emphasized baseball's push to hire more minorities.

Sunday's tributes also will put a spotlight on an uncomfortable question for baseball: Is Robinson's legacy within the game fading?

The percentage of African-Americans in the majors has dropped sharply during the last decade and now is the lowest it has been since the 1960s—8.3%, or 72 players on opening-day rosters, according to a USA TODAY study that includes injured players.

The percentage of blacks in key front-office, managing and coaching positions hasn't increased during the last decade. Even MLB's central office, with about 470 employees mostly in New York, has a smaller percentage of blacks than it did in 1997. However, two of MLB's five executive vice presidents—positions created since 1997—are black.

Robinson, who kept crusading for equal opportunity for the disadvantaged after his playing career ended in 1956, probably would not accept this situation, his widow says.

"He was always impatient for change and a fighter for change," Rachel Robinson says. "He would think the struggle is still on, and he would not be satisfied with where we are."

"Are we where we should be? No. We've got a lot of work to do," says Jimmie Lee Solomon, MLB executive vice president for baseball operations and an African-American. "Are we working on it? Yeah, we're working hard on it."

A Harris Interactive survey released in January found only 7% of African-American adults said baseball was their favorite sport. This comes at a time of growth for other minorities on the field; nearly one in three MLB players is Latino or Asian. Their increased presence has pushed the overall percentage of minority players to 40.5% this year, the highest ever.

—*Mike Dodd*

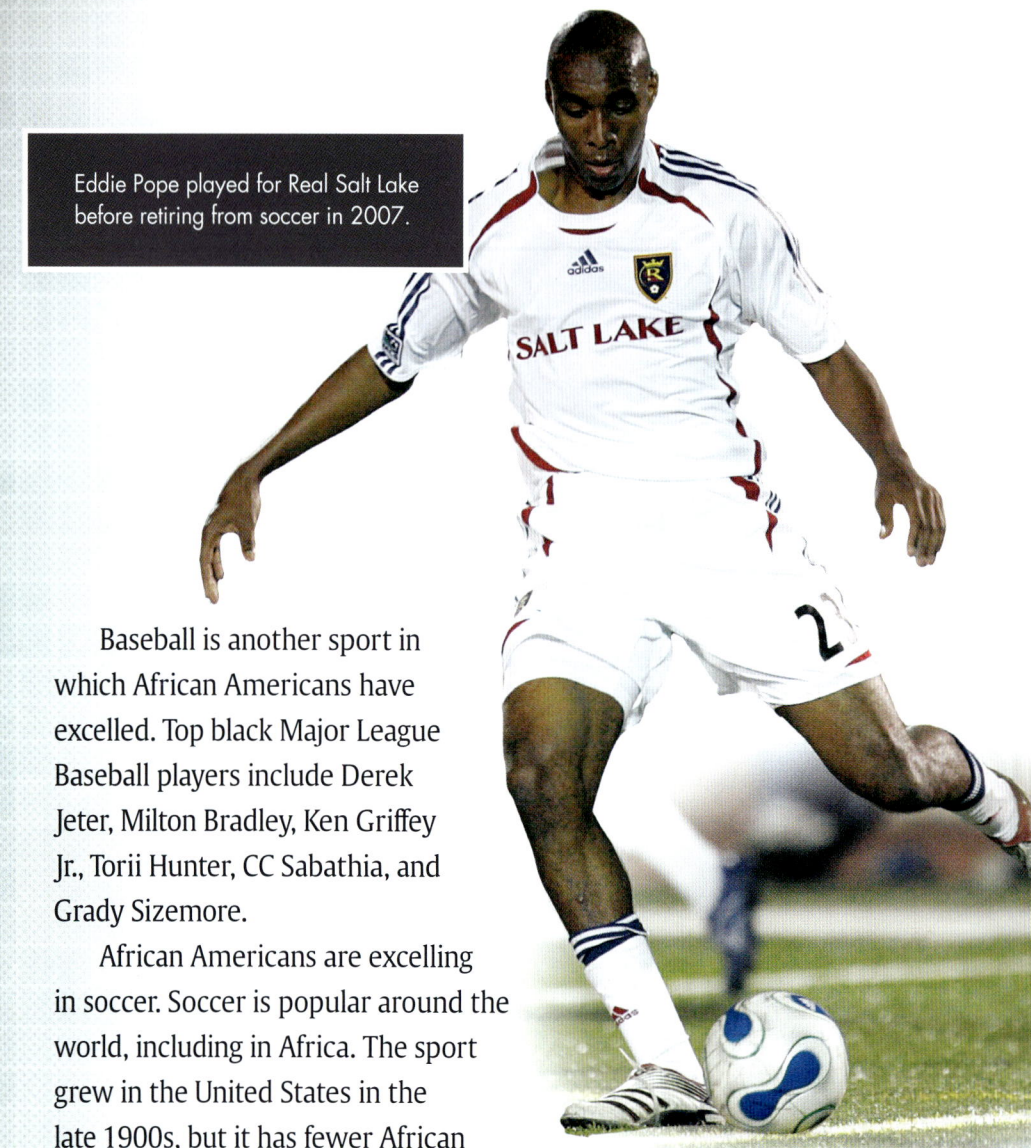

Eddie Pope played for Real Salt Lake before retiring from soccer in 2007.

Baseball is another sport in which African Americans have excelled. Top black Major League Baseball players include Derek Jeter, Milton Bradley, Ken Griffey Jr., Torii Hunter, CC Sabathia, and Grady Sizemore.

African Americans are excelling in soccer. Soccer is popular around the world, including in Africa. The sport grew in the United States in the late 1900s, but it has fewer African American players than basketball, football, or baseball. One black U.S. soccer superstar is Eddie Pope. Pope spent eleven years in Major League Soccer. He also played for the United States in the World Cup, an international soccer tournament. Macoumba Kandji, an immigrant to the United States from Senegal, became a Major League Soccer player in 2006.

THE AFRICAN AMERICAN EXPERIENCE

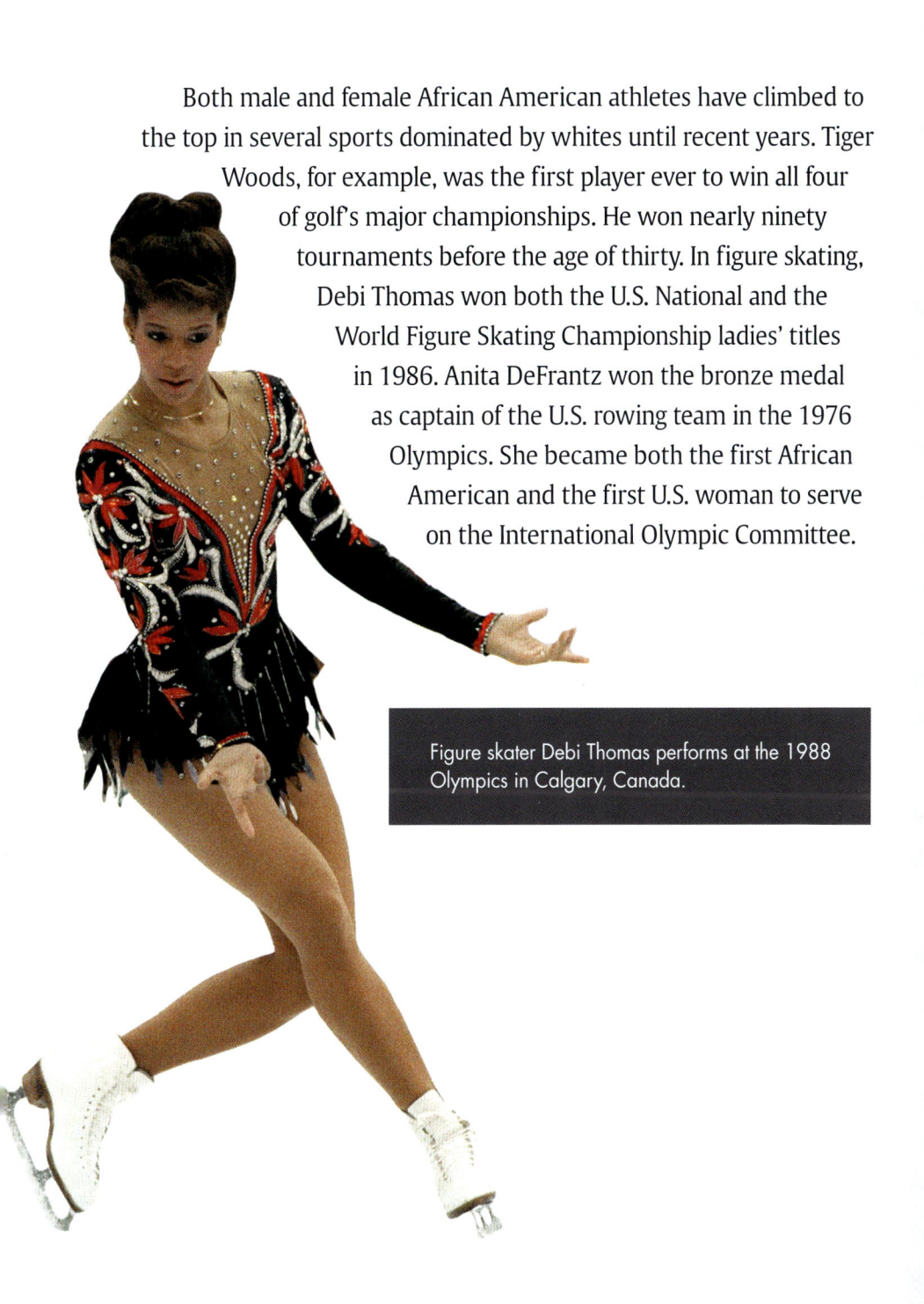

Both male and female African American athletes have climbed to the top in several sports dominated by whites until recent years. Tiger Woods, for example, was the first player ever to win all four of golf's major championships. He won nearly ninety tournaments before the age of thirty. In figure skating, Debi Thomas won both the U.S. National and the World Figure Skating Championship ladies' titles in 1986. Anita DeFrantz won the bronze medal as captain of the U.S. rowing team in the 1976 Olympics. She became both the first African American and the first U.S. woman to serve on the International Olympic Committee.

Figure skater Debi Thomas performs at the 1988 Olympics in Calgary, Canada.

ON THE PLAYING FIELD • 41

CHAPTER 4:
RELIGION

African Americans belong to diverse religions. Over hundreds of years, their religious practices have changed dramatically. But religion remains important to many African Americans.

A woman sings and dances in front of a choir at a church in California.

RELIGION AND SLAVERY

Africans brought many religions with them when they came to the United States as slaves. Each African ethnic group had a unique religion. Some of these religions are animist. Animists believe spirits inhabit natural places, beings, things, and the everyday world. Music and dance play a big role in many traditional African religions. In addition, many Africans taken as slaves were Muslims.

42 · **THE AFRICAN AMERICAN EXPERIENCE**

It was difficult for people torn from their roots to practice their religions in the United States. Religious rituals often depend on social relationships. So the loss of family and community made it hard to hold on to rituals. Also, most slave owners forbade slaves to practice any religion besides Christianity. Some enslaved Africans secretly preserved some African religious rituals. But many more adopted Christianity. Some brought elements of their African religions to their new faith.

White southern preachers worked hard to convert slaves to Christianity. Many preachers told slaves that they had to obey their masters. They said obedience was a slave's only path to heaven. Many slave owners wanted their slaves to hear this message. But owners were afraid that slaves who gathered to worship on their own would plot rebellion or escape. So masters insisted that they and their slaves worship in the same church.

Still, some slaves found ways to meet and worship in secret. At these secret meetings, slaves sang and chanted, often mixing Christianity with African traditions. Many of the songs and chants had double meanings. The words described hope for salvation for African Americans.

USA TODAY Snapshots®

Keeping the faith

By denomination, the percentage of people who say religion is very important to their lives:

Denomination	Percentage
Black Protestant	85%
White evangelical Protestant	79%
Muslim	72%
Catholic	49%
White mainline Protestant	36%
Religiously unaffiliated	10%

Source: 2007 Pew Research Center survey of Muslim Americans and Pew Global Attitudes project surveys from 2005 and 2006; margin of error ranging from ± 5 to 9 percentage points.

By Tracey Wong Briggs and Veronica Salazar, USA TODAY, 2007

RELIGION • 43

RELIGION, NORTHERN STYLE

Even before the Civil War, many free African Americans lived in northern states. Free blacks in the North were mostly Christian.

Christian churches in the North preached about the equality of blacks and whites. Many northern churches worked to end slavery. They offered shelter, transport, food, and other help to people who escaped slavery.

Not all northern Christians wanted to end slavery. Some churches split over this disagreement. The Free Methodist Church, for example, split from the Methodist Episcopal Church in 1860. Methodists who wanted to end slavery founded the Free Methodist Church.

Blacks in the North often attended church alongside white people. But some churches discriminated against African Americans. These churches ordered blacks to sit in separate areas. By the early 1800s, some northern blacks started their own churches to avoid such discrimination. In 1816 African Americans in Pennsylvania founded the nation's first independent black Christian denomination. It was called the African Methodist Episcopal (AME) Church.

Soon several African American churches sprang up around New England. Some of these churches had schools for black children. Some published newspapers. Many served as the center of social life for the African American community.

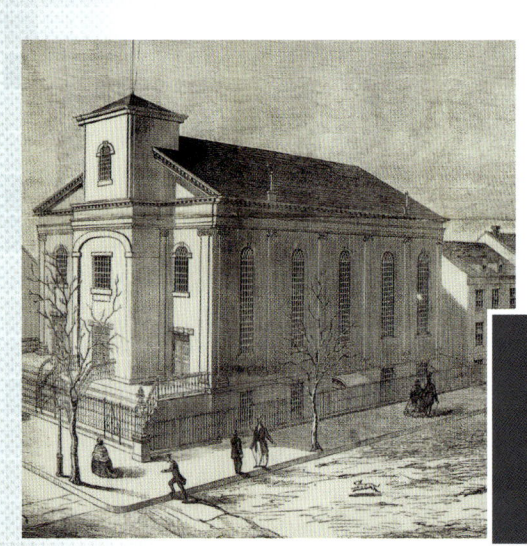

This drawing shows the African Methodist Episcopal Zion Church in New York in the late 1800s. It was one of the largest African American churches after the Civil War.

44 · THE AFRICAN AMERICAN EXPERIENCE

Religion and Civil Rights

The most famous U.S. civil rights leader, Martin Luther King Jr., was a Christian preacher. In 1957 King formed an organization called the Southern Christian Leadership Conference (SCLC) to seek equal rights for African Americans. King and the SCLC used nonviolent means to protest racial discrimination. They organized peaceful demonstrations and boycotts. (In a boycott, people refuse to deal with an organization or company in hopes of changing its practices.) In the 1950s and 1960s, the SCLC also registered black voters and demanded equal educational opportunities for blacks. The SCLC is still active in the twenty-first century.

AFTER SLAVERY

After the Civil War, four million slaves became free. Most sought new homes, jobs, schools, and churches. Hundreds of thousands joined African American Christian churches.

In these churches, the newly free people worshipped as they always had. They included some African rituals in their worship. They sang and danced. Most black churchgoers could not read. They memorized scripture and told Bible stories to spread Christian teachings.

Many northern churches wanted to help the freed African Americans adjust to their new life. Some collected money. Some built schools and helped in other ways. Some northern Christians disapproved of the new southern black churches. They thought the southern churches permitted too much dancing, singing, and storytelling.

RELIGION • 45

Church members participate in a service at a Baptist church in Georgia in 2007. About twelve million African Americans are Baptists.

Black churches kept growing in different ways in the North and the South. Modern southern black churches still do more singing and clapping. Modern northern churches focus more on Bible reading. But across the United States, Christianity remains an important part of African American culture.

In the early 2000s, some African American Christians attend integrated churches. Others attend mostly black churches. The church is the social center of many African American communities. These churches often work to end racism. Many also focus on fighting poverty,

USA TODAY Snapshots®

Black History Month

Pushing back poverty
Poverty rate for blacks:

- 1985: **31.4%**
- 2005: **24.9%**

Source: Census Bureau By David Stuckey and Sam Ward, USA TODAY, 2007

46 • THE AFRICAN AMERICAN EXPERIENCE

USA TODAY CULTURAL MOSAIC

which affects African American communities more than European American ones. For example, the churches might help people get housing and jobs or work to end drug dealing or gang violence.

ISLAM

Up to 20 percent of early African Americans may have been Muslims. Slavery largely destroyed this heritage. However, many recent African immigrants to the United States practice Islam. Islam is a widespread religion in Africa. People who practice Islam are called Muslims.

The word *Islam* means "surrender to the will of Allah." *Allah* is the word for "God." Muslims believe that Allah gave messages to his prophet (spiritual spokesperson) Muhammad through the angel Gabriel in the A.D. 600s. The holy scriptures of the Quran contain these messages.

Muslims around the world strive to fulfill five central duties. These are called the five pillars of Islam. They include declaring faith in Allah and Muhammad; praying five times daily; fasting from sunrise to sunset during the holy month of Ramadan; giving charity; and traveling to the holy city of Mecca, Saudi Arabia, once in a lifetime, if possible. Friday is the day of worship for Muslims.

In addition to the five pillars, most U.S. Muslims follow Islamic customs such as not eating pork or drinking alcohol. Islam encourages both men and women to wear modest clothing in public. Some women also cover their hair with head scarves.

Muslim women attend a prayer service in Minnesota in 2009. Some Muslim women cover their hair in public.

RELIGION • 47

Nation of Islam

The Nation of Islam is a uniquely African American religion. People who follow this religion often call themselves Black Muslims. The Nation of Islam began in Detroit, Michigan, in the early 1930s. Its goal is to improve the lives of black men and women. Some Black Muslims believe that this means African Americans should have their own country. Others believe it means they deserve better treatment within the United States. Black Muslims worship Allah. They believe that W. D. Fard, the Nation of Islam's founder, was Allah on Earth. Other Muslims do not believe this. Louis Farrakhan *(above)* has been the leader of the Nation of Islam since 1978.

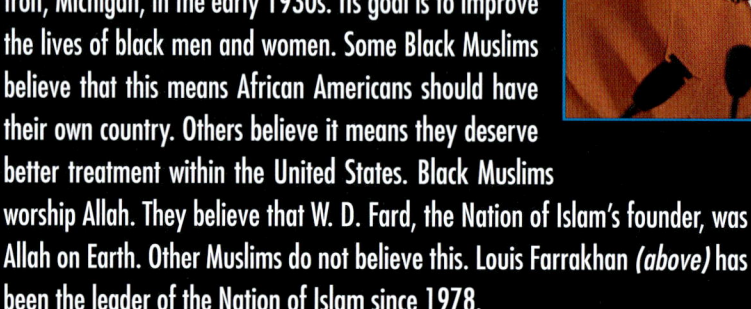

Many U.S. Muslims have faced discrimination because their practices stand out in U.S. society. Since September 11, 2001, when radical Muslim terrorists carried out deadly attacks in the United States, Muslim Americans have faced even greater discrimination.

U.S. Muslims have spoken out against terrorism. They have explained that radicals and terrorists do not represent their views. However, some non-Muslim Americans continue to treat U.S. Muslims unfairly. This discrimination has included violence and death threats. Muslim Americans find they must work very hard to earn fair treatment in many parts of the nation.

48 · **THE AFRICAN AMERICAN EXPERIENCE**

November 7, 2001

From the Pages of USA TODAY

War is a conflict for America's Muslim teens

ATLANTA—Ahmed El-Helw, an intense young man who talks passionately and to the point, has a different perspective on Sept. 11 from most of his classmates at Georgia Tech. The 18-year-old freshman says he was shocked and saddened by the terrorist attacks. But he has been even more disturbed by subsequent events.

Muslim youths in the USA are watching the war on terrorism from a complicated, often tortured vantage point. They say they have felt the soul-searing tug of competing loyalties and have seen their beloved religion distorted by both the nation's enemies and its media.

Many of these young people say their non-Muslim peers have stereotyped them as disloyal to the United States or dangerous because of the terrorist attacks. Some young Muslims say they have changed their appearance or lifestyles to avoid being harassed.

Several common themes emerged in interviews with young Muslims. All of them deplore the terrorist attacks, but their opinions vary over the U.S. military response.

"I think the American people really need to take a good look at U.S. government policy," says Zaynab Ansari, 24, who is majoring in Arabic and Islamic studies at Georgia Perimeter College near Atlanta. "U.S. policy toward Palestine has been greatly biased in favor of Israel."

Ansari's mother is African-American, her father Lebanese. She discusses the war on terrorism during a recent open house at [the mosque, or house of worship, her family attends].

Many parents from the mosque have been visiting their children's schools trying to help non-Muslims gain a better understanding of Islam. They say they are trying to correct what many young Muslims perceive as a distortion of Islam by U.S. media.

Atlanta has more than 20 mosques with about 75,000 members—about 40% of them African-American. Nationally, a study this year by the Council on American-Islamic Relations and the Hartford Institute for Religious Research found that 30% of those who attend mosques regularly are African-American and 25% are of Arab descent.

Some young black Muslims say their loyalty has been questioned since Sept. 11—even by other African-Americans—and that they have been subjected to ... religious slights.

—Larry Copeland

CHAPTER 5:

CELEBRATING AFRICAN AMERICAN CULTURE

Holidays, festivals, and other celebrations are times for African American families to come together. Often three or even four generations of a family will gather to celebrate important events. Music and food are key ingredients of any African American celebration.

Many holidays reflect religious beliefs. Others are ways of honoring ancestors and their struggles.

Like Americans of all backgrounds, African Americans celebrate all sorts of holidays, depending on their religion, location, and preference. Birthdays, graduations, and weddings are special events.

Many African American families celebrate holidays with food, such as this family eating a turkey dinner at Christmas.

50 · THE AFRICAN AMERICAN EXPERIENCE

Religious celebrations such as Christmas and Easter often feature family gatherings with lots of food. Large family reunions are popular among some black Americans. Some celebrate their African roots during the holiday of Kwanzaa.

CHRISTMAS

Christmas is the biggest holiday of the year for many African Americans. Christians celebrate this day as the birthday of Jesus Christ. But even families who are not very religious often celebrate Christmas as a time of family togetherness.

People often travel long distances for Christmas. In African American families, adult sons and daughters commonly bring their own children, if they have them, to spend the holiday with grandparents, aunts, uncles, and cousins. Typically, families host out-of-town relatives for several days around December 25.

African Americans participate in many Christmas activities. Families decorate their homes. They trim Christmas trees. They have parties with

This family opens presents to celebrate Christmas. Trimming a Christmas tree and gathering for a family meal are also important holiday activities for many African American families.

CELEBRATING AFRICAN AMERICAN CULTURE • 51

special food. And they exchange gifts. Christian families attend church services together. Most African American families share a big Christmas meal.

Some traditional Christmas symbols carry extra meaning for African Americans. For example, a Christmas star represents the star that guided three wise men to the baby Jesus Christ. In African American culture, a star also symbolizes the North Star. This bright star guided thousands of escaping slaves northward to freedom from the South.

Black Nativity

Attending a production of *Black Nativity* is a favorite holiday tradition for Americans of many races. Langston Hughes (1902–1967) wrote this play. It sets the story of Jesus's birth to gospel music. During the weeks leading up to Christmas, churches and theater groups across the United States put on this beloved performance.

This performance of *Black Nativity* took place in Saint Paul, Minnesota.

CELEBRATING AFRICAN CULTURE

Some African Americans want to do more than include symbols of their history in Christmas celebrations. They want to actively celebrate their African roots.

That is the purpose of Kwanzaa. This seven-day celebration begins each year on the day after Christmas. It lasts from December 26 to January 1. The word *kwanzaa* means "first fruits" in the East African language of Swahili. But the holiday didn't come from Africa. A university professor invented it in the United States in 1966.

During Kwanzaa, African American families set up a special altar. On it, they place a kinara (candleholder with seven candles). Three of the candles are green. They represent Earth. Three candles are red. They represent the blood spilled in African American history. The seventh candle is black. It represents the

Children and adults take part in a Kwanzaa celebration at a museum in New Jersey.

December 27, 2002

From the Pages of USA TODAY
Kwanzaa's principles embrace solid values

What's not to love about Kwanzaa, the African-American celebration of heritage, family and community that began Thursday and runs through New Year's Day? After Christmas' mad rush, it offers an oasis of calm and introspection, an alternative to the season's often overpowering commercialism.

Kwanzaa was created in 1966 by California black studies scholar Maulana Karenga, who incorporated elements of African harvest festivals into a unique observance celebrated today by more than 18 million people in the USA.

Because Kwanzaa isn't a religious holiday and was never meant to replace Christmas, many black families celebrate both, allowing Kwanzaa's seven-branched candleholder, called a kinara, to occupy a special place alongside their Christmas tree. During each day of Kwanzaa, a candle is lit to symbolize one of the seven principles that serve as the day's message: unity, self-deter-

power of the African American people. On the first night of Kwanzaa, a family lights one candle. Each following night, the family lights one more candle. On the final night, all seven candles burn.

On each day of Kwanzaa, families celebrate a different life principle. The first day honors unity. The second day celebrates self-determination. The third day highlights work and responsibility. The fourth day focuses on cooperative economics (spending money within one's own community). The fifth day is reserved for thinking about life's purpose. The sixth day honors creativity. And on the seventh day, people focus on their faith.

mination, collective work and responsibility, cooperative economics, purpose, creativity and faith.

Adhering to the principles "requires us to make our conduct correspond to our convictions," says Tulivu Jadi, assistant director of the African American Cultural Center, Kwanzaa's founding organization. "It's an ongoing challenge to make them merge."

Guests exchange simple gifts, preferably educational items such as books or African-inspired objects. In keeping with Kwanzaa's tenets, gifts other than books should be homemade. The holiday comes to a heady climax on Tuesday, when people share the foods, music, art, dance and stories of their heritage at a huge feast.

Kwanzaa's growing popularity has raised concerns that it is becoming too mainstream (it's been an official "Hallmark holiday" for a decade). To prevent commercial co-option, those who love the holiday must resist the blitz for black dollars.

Kwanzaa, in fact, is an excellent occasion for African-Americans to practice "muscular black pride," says Eric V. Copage, author of a book about the holiday. "It's a time to examine the actions that pride leads us to take, and to reflect on what it means to be a black man or woman, to contemplate who we are and where we're going."

I'll be joining the millions taking part in that sacred journey. When I light the kinara's red, black and green candles with my family and pause to thank my ancestors for their gifts, I am passing on the values of past generations and pledging myself to the promise of a better future. Ideally, the principles of Kwanzaa—and its warm spirit—will be carried forward throughout the year by all who have embraced this young holiday.

—Desda Moss

Families usually plan special activities for all seven days. Many families use Kwanzaa to teach children about their African heritage. Children learn about relatives who have died. They also learn about famous African Americans. All who celebrate Kwanzaa do it to recognize the importance of the past in shaping their future.

Kwanzaa occasionally sparks conflict within communities. Some white Americans consider it a minor made-up holiday. They don't take Kwanzaa celebrations seriously, nor do they want schools to teach children about the holiday. Even African Americans have varying attitudes about Kwanzaa. Some African Americans who celebrate

Kwanzaa look down on those who don't and vice versa. Nevertheless, the holiday remains important for those who choose to celebrate their African roots in this particular way.

NAMING CEREMONIES

Some African American families follow African traditions in naming children. In most parts of Africa, choosing a baby's name is a sacred activity. Many Africans believe that a person's name helps shape his or her future. So choosing the correct name for a child is important. Naming often involves the entire community. Sometimes a village elder will choose the name.

Some African American families follow this example. They take great care in naming each baby. They may choose the name of an admired relative or ancestor. Other families choose African names with special meanings.

Once a family chooses a name, it may hold a naming ceremony. Such ceremonies are common throughout Africa. In the United States, a family may base its naming ceremony on traditions of the region it comes from.

Usually a naming ceremony takes place during the first week of an infant's life. It may be an elaborate event at a rented banquet room. Or it may be a simple party at someone's home. The parents and grandparents are the most important participants. Godparents, adults chosen by the parents to play a special role in the child's life, are guests of honor. Other relatives join the celebration too. The family plans activities to welcome a child into the world. A family elder typically speaks about the family's history. The parents and grandparents speak about their wishes for the child's future. Brothers, sisters, or cousins of the new baby may play an instrument or read a poem.

Fasting and Celebrating

Each year during the holy month of Ramadan, African American Muslims fast. (Because Islam follows a lunar, or moon, calendar, not the solar calendar, Ramadan falls on different dates every year.) The month celebrates the time when the prophet Muhammad began to receive the words of God. Muslims do not eat or drink anything from sunup until sundown for all of Ramadan. Then, on the first day of the next month, they celebrate Eid-al-Fitr. This holiday marks the end of the fasting month. Muslims begin this day with a sweet breakfast and celebrate for the rest of the day. They dress up to attend the special Eid prayer at their neighborhood mosque. But first, they give a gift of money or food to the poor. After the prayer service, family members exchange gifts. In some communities, Eid-al-Fitr lasts up to three days.

These women make preparations to celebrate Eid-al-Fitr in New Jersey.

Sometimes naming ceremonies occur when an adult changes his or her name. Some African Americans decide to change from their given names to chosen African names after learning about their African history. They feel that changing names recognizes the importance of their African heritage. Sometimes an entire family will adopt African names together. When African Americans adopt African names, they may continue to use their birth names. Or they may completely switch to their African names.

CELEBRATING AFRICAN AMERICAN CULTURE • 57

Soul food—such as this meal of corn bread, barbecue ribs, collard greens, and macaroni and cheese—is popular in the South.

USA TODAY CULTURAL MOSAIC

CHAPTER 6:
FOOD

Most African Americans eat the same varied diet that other Americans eat. This diet might include a cheeseburger and fries one day, sushi the next day, and pizza another day. Some African Americans maintain the food traditions of their ancestors. Many African American recipes and customs began in the days of slavery.

SLAVE MEALS

U.S. slave owners generally fed their African slaves poorly. Often slaves got only the meat scraps that their masters wouldn't eat. For instance, if a slave-owning family ate roast pork, the pig's feet would go to the slaves. While the white family ate ham, the slaves would get the ham hock, or bony leg joint. Chitterlings, often called chitlins (pig intestines), also commonly went to slaves.

Along with meat scraps, slaves received leftover crops—often corn—from the land they worked. If allowed, slaves would grow other crops to eat. They often grew collards (leafy greens related to cabbage and broccoli). Collards are easy to grow and very nutritious. Sometimes slaves grew vegetables from Africa, such as sweet potatoes and okra.

A slave family typically had one pot and an open fire for cooking. In this the family first cooked meat scraps. Then they would add corn, collards, or whatever vegetables they had. They often made bread or porridge out of cornmeal too.

Versatile Cornmeal

Cornmeal is a versatile (easy to adapt) ingredient. People use it to make corn bread in a cast iron skillet over an open fire or baked in an oven. The batter formed into patties on a griddle makes hoecakes. Deep-fried balls of the batter are called hush puppies. Coarsely ground cornmeal, or hominy, can be boiled to make grits *(right)*. Many people like to eat this porridgelike dish with butter and sugar for breakfast. Some cooks coat fish or meat in a cornmeal mix before frying it. Cornmeal stuffing is good in a Thanksgiving turkey.

The end of U.S. slavery freed African Americans from the diets their masters forced on them. But blacks were usually too poor to change their menu much. In the late 1800s and early 1900s, most African Americans ate the same foods that all poor southerners ate. This diet included ham hocks, pigs' feet, and collard greens. It also included lima beans, cowpeas (black-eyed peas), and green beans. Corn and cornmeal remained dietary staples (common and important foods).

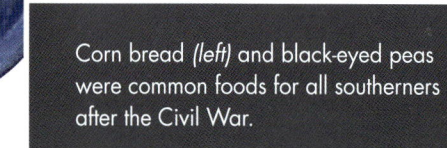

Corn bread *(left)* and black-eyed peas were common foods for all southerners after the Civil War.

60 · THE AFRICAN AMERICAN EXPERIENCE

Pork and chicken were favorite meats in the South. But poor black people, just like poor white people, could not afford to be picky. They caught or trapped whatever meat they could to feed their families. When southerners couldn't afford pork or chicken, they cooked raccoons, opossums, rabbits, squirrels, catfish, frogs, crayfish (small freshwater lobsters), and turtles.

FROM SOUTHERN FOOD TO SOUL FOOD

For many decades after the Civil War, the diet of poor southerners changed little. But different areas of the South did have varying regional cuisines.

For example, Spanish and French settlers in Louisiana created a cuisine called Creole. Creole food uses many common southern ingredients, but it also features spicy tomato sauces and rich stews. In rice-growing states such as North and South Carolina, people ate more rice and less corn. And barbecue was popular in many areas. To barbecue meat, people cook it slowly over an open fire. The various regions of the South developed unique sauces and spices. In some regions, barbecued meat is highly spiced and eaten dry. In other areas, it's slathered with sweet, spicy sauce.

Red beans and rice is a standard Creole dish.

In the 1940s, many southern blacks moved north in search of jobs. They brought their food tastes with them to cities such as New York, Chicago, and Detroit. Inexpensive restaurants sprang up around the neighborhoods where newly arrived African Americans lived. These restaurants served southern specialties such as fried chicken, corn bread, mashed potatoes, and chitlin gravy. The restaurants served mainly neighborhood families. But they also introduced new flavors to northerners. Most established northerners had never heard of such dishes as barbecue ribs, corn bread, or grits. Since blacks introduced these foods, northerners assumed they were African American foods.

By the 1960s, African Americans were using the word *soul* to describe their culture. African American music was soul music,

This California restaurant serves soul food such as fried chicken, gravy, and waffles. Soul food restaurants are common in bigger cities across the United States.

and African American food became known as soul food. Soul food restaurants became popular with black and white customers in cities across the United States. These restaurants served heaping helpings of fried chicken, macaroni and cheese, biscuits and gravy, and barbecue ribs.

AFRICAN IMMIGRANT FOOD

Africans who immigrated to the United States in the late 1900s and early 2000s brought their native cuisines with them. Africa is a huge continent and is home to many cooking styles. Slow-cooked stews of spiced meat and vegetables are popular in many parts of Africa. Some African dishes use ingredients common in the southern United States. For instance, cowpeas, okra, and tomatoes appear in many African soups and stews. Peanuts, hot peppers, and lentils are also common.

Some African immigrants brought tastes for foods considered exotic in the United States. In Nigeria the hosts at a feast serve a goat's head to important guests. Nigerians have settled in U.S. cities such as Houston, Texas, and Washington, D.C. Butchers in these cities have begun selling goats' heads. U.S. butcher shops that serve African immigrants may also sell intestines and stomachs from lambs and other animals. These meats are considered delicacies (rare and special treats) in several parts of Africa.

Islamic law describes specific ways to slaughter animals: halal (permitted) and haram (forbidden). Many U.S. cities have halal butchers.

Thanks to African immigrants, most large U.S. cities have African restaurants. At an Ethiopian restaurant, you can experience family-style dining with no silverware. Servers place large platters of food and baskets of flat, spongy bread called injera in the middle of the table.

West African Peanut Soup

This hearty peanut and tomato soup is a favorite in western African countries.

INGREDIENTS

2 tablespoons olive oil
2 medium onions, chopped
2 large red bell peppers, chopped
4 cloves garlic, minced
1 28-ounce can crushed tomatoes, with liquid
8 cups vegetable broth
¼ teaspoon black pepper
¼ teaspoon chili powder (optional)
½ cup uncooked brown rice
⅔ cup extra crunchy peanut butter
1 tablespoon lemon or lime juice
2 tablespoons chopped fresh cilantro
1 to 2 cups chopped fresh dark leafy greens, such as spinach, collards, or kale
cayenne pepper to taste

PREPARATION

1. Heat oil in a large soup kettle over medium-high heat. Cook onions and bell peppers until lightly browned and tender. Stir in garlic when onions and peppers are almost done to prevent burning. Stir in tomatoes, broth, black pepper, and chili powder.
2. Reduce heat to low and simmer, uncovered, for 30 minutes.
3. Stir in rice, cover, and simmer another 30 minutes, or until rice is tender.
4. Stir in peanut butter until well blended. Stir in remaining ingredients, then serve.

Makes 6 to 8 servings

This brother and sister own an Ethiopian restaurant in Sacramento, California. They are enjoying a traditional Ethiopian meal with a platter of different foods, bread, wine, and spiced tea.

Guests tear off pieces of bread and use the bread to scoop up the main dishes. The main dishes are typically stews made from meat, beans, vegetables, and spices. A South African restaurant may serve bobotie. This is a kind of meat loaf. A cook mixes ground beef or lamb with eggs, dried apricots, raisins, apples, onions, and spices such as curry powder and turmeric. At a Ghanaian restaurant, you can try foo-foo or banku. Both are everyday dishes from Ghana. They are a thick paste or dough made of boiled and pounded starchy root vegetables (foo-foo) or cornmeal (banku) and served with soup.

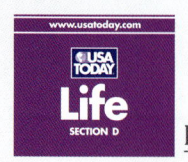

December 20, 2006

From the Pages of USA TODAY

The recipe is remembrance; A traditional treat of black Americans has a loving curator in Elbert Mackey

Family food traditions are as much a part of the holidays as wrapping paper and jingle bells. For Elbert Mackey, this means whipping up a batch of tea cakes—golden-brown, circle-shaped cookies with a hint of vanilla and nutmeg.

To be honest, Mackey says, he doesn't limit his much-loved recipe to the Christmas season. But in a time of year when preparing food also means sharing family stories and a bit of yourself, his passion for tea cakes takes on added meaning.

Mackey, 57, owner of an Austin, Texas, medical-equipment repair business, is trying to preserve the tea cake recipes that were often a favorite in African-American homes before the advent of convenience foods. He also wants to collect stories, poems and remembrances associated with this dessert.

He launched The Tea Cake Project (www.TeacakeProject.com) this fall to solicit recipes and stories that he hopes to include in a cookbook next year.

"Occasionally in Southern cookbooks you see a recipe here or there, but nothing dedicated to tea cakes, and nothing unique to African-Americans," Mackey says. "These little bites of heaven are disappearing."

Tea cakes were introduced to the [American] Colonies by the British,

THE MELTING POT

One thing that established African Americans and recent African immigrants have in common is the family meal. Both groups love to share meals with extended family. In Africa, gathering many generations together for meals is a common tradition. U.S. slaves continued this tradition as best they could. Large family meals have who served sweet cookies or cakes with afternoon tea or with the more formal "high tea" later in the day, says Atlanta-based food editor and teatime historian Millie Coleman, author of *The South's Legendary Frances Virginia Tea Room Cookbook*.

During the 1800s, in regions of the South with a strong Scots-Irish or British background, the tea cake tradition carried on, except that the standard recipe became more of a sweet cookie, Coleman says. The term also expanded to include a variety of cookies and cakes served with tea, she explains.

Tea cakes were not a slave food, says food historian Jessica Harris, author of *The Welcome Table: African-American Heritage Cooking*. "The white flour is an ingredient that slaves would not have had access to. And when it's sweetened with refined white sugar, you know it's relatively recent," she says.

Still, over time and throughout the South, many African-Americans adopted the food as their own, sometimes as a snack, other times as a treat for special occasions, especially Easter and Christmas, says Mackey.

Because the basic ingredients—flour, eggs, milk, sugar—were relatively inexpensive household staples, tea cakes could be enjoyed by families of limited economic means, he says. "Along the way, cooks would add their own special ingredients, such as molasses, grated lemon rind, various spices and flavoring. Something simple was turned into something wonderful," he says.

—Michelle Healy

Tea cakes have long been popular with African American families.

always been an important part of African American life. These meals often take place after church on Sundays. That's when steaming platters of home-cooked soul food fill the tables in many black households.

The traditional African American menu has changed a little in recent years. Many soul food dishes—such as biscuits with gravy, macaroni and cheese, and fried chicken—are high in fat and salt.

Aunt Maggie's Old-Fashioned Tea Cakes

Tea cakes have been called the national cookies of African Americans. Vanilla and nutmeg give these treats their distinctive flavor. This recipe makes delicious tea cakes just like those of Elbert Mackey's Aunt Maggie.

INGREDIENTS

- 1 cup butter-flavored shortening
- 2 cups granulated sugar
- 4 eggs, lightly beaten
- 1 tablespoon evaporated milk
- ½ tablespoon vanilla extract
- 4 cups all-purpose flour
- 4 teaspoons baking powder
- ¼ teaspoon ground nutmeg

PREPARATION

1. Preheat oven to 350°F. In a large bowl, mix shortening and sugar until creamy. Add eggs, milk, and vanilla.
2. In another bowl, sift together flour, baking powder, and nutmeg. Add dry ingredients to the batter 1 cup at a time and mix well. Dough will be slightly stiff. Chill dough for at least 1 hour.
3. Spray an ice cream scoop with vegetable oil spray, and scoop out dough. Place dough scoops on an ungreased cookie sheet, and bake for about 10 minutes, or until tea cakes are lightly browned and tops begin to crack.
4. Watch carefully so tea cakes don't get too brown. Let them cool for a few minutes before removing to a rack. Transfer to a serving dish. Store leftovers in an airtight container for 3 to 5 days.

Makes 12 to 15 tea cakes

Eating a lot of salty, high-fat food can cause illnesses such as diabetes and heart disease. In fact, studies show that both of those illnesses are more common among African Americans than among white Americans.

For better health, many African Americans are eating leaner meat, fresh fruit, and vegetables. Luckily, many ingredients found in traditional African American cooking are healthy. For instance, greens and beans are packed with nutrients. When cooked in animal fat, these foods are problematic. So African Americans, like many other Americans, are improving their diets by cooking differently. For example, people may steam greens and vegetables and fry with vegetable oils instead of animal fat. African Americans hope such changes will lead to healthier lives.

This family shares a meal.

FAMOUS AFRICAN AMERICANS

Maya Angelou (b. 1928)

Maya Angelou is an author, poet, playwright, performer, and director. She was born in Saint Louis, Missouri, on April 4, 1928. She studied dance and drama and toured Europe with the opera *Porgy and Bess* in 1954 and 1955. By the late 1950s, she was writing, acting, and living in New York City. Angelou published her autobiography, *I Know Why the Caged Bird Sings*, in 1970. Since then she has become a highly honored U.S. writer. She has published more than thirty books and has directed several movies and television shows. She received the National Medal of Arts in 2000.

Charles Drew (1904–1950)

Charles Drew invented the blood bank. This system for storing donated blood has saved millions of lives. Drew was born in Washington, D.C., on June 3, 1904. He was the oldest of five children. He discovered that when plasma (a clear yellowish fluid component of blood) is separated from the rest of the blood, the blood can be stored for a long time. This discovery allowed doctors to store donated blood for people who needed extra due to sickness or injury. The first blood bank was used in World War II (1939–1945). Later, Drew started and directed the American Red Cross Blood Bank. In 1950 he was killed in a car crash.

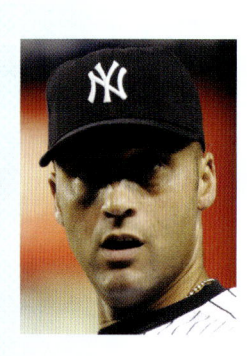

Derek Jeter (b. 1974)

New York Yankees shortstop Derek Jeter is a baseball superstar. Jeter was born in New Jersey. When Jeter was in high school, many people thought he was the nation's best youth baseball player. In 1992 the New York Yankees drafted him. He has helped the Yankees win five World Series titles. He has also played in Major League Baseball's All-Star game ten times. Fans admire his incredible plays. Jeter has also earned respect for his community service. In 2009 *Sports Illustrated* magazine named Jeter Sportsman of the Year.

Queen Latifah (b. 1970)
Queen Latifah was one of the first female rap stars. She was born Dana Owens on March 18, 1970, in Newark, New Jersey. She broke into the music world at the age of eighteen when she released her first single, "Wrath of My Madness." A year later, she released the chart-topping album *All Hail the Queen*. In the 1990s, she released three more hip-hop albums. She also appears in and produces movies and has had her own talk show, *The Queen Latifah Show*.

Barack Obama (b. 1961)
President Barack Obama is the first African-American U.S. president. Obama grew up in Hawaii and in Indonesia. After graduating from Columbia University and Harvard Law School, he moved to Chicago and worked as a lawyer. In 2004 he won a landslide election to the U.S. Senate. He helped pass a law to assist people in paying for college. Americans elected him president in 2008. As president he has worked to create jobs and to reform the U.S. health care system.

Rosa Parks (1913–2005)
Rosa Parks was born on February 4, 1913, in Tuskegee, Alabama. On December 1, 1955, on her way home from a day's work at a Montgomery department store, Parks was arrested and fined for not giving up her bus seat. Her action led to a citywide bus boycott by African Americans. The boycott lasted for 381 days. It brought world attention to racial discrimination in the United States. Near the end of the boycott, the U.S. Supreme Court outlawed all bus segregation. In 1996 Parks received the Presidential Medal of Freedom. She received a Congressional Gold Medal in 1999 and died in 2005.

Oprah Winfrey (b. 1954)
Oprah Winfrey is one of the world's best-known entertainers and media executives. She was also the first African American billionaire. Winfrey was born in Kosciusko, Mississippi, on January 29, 1954. She started her media career as a radio news reporter. *The Oprah Winfrey Show* first aired nationally in 1986. It made her one of the world's most famous faces. Winfrey uses her popularity and wealth to work for many causes, including improving education and ending child abuse.

EXPLORE YOUR HERITAGE

Where did your family come from? Who are your relatives, and where do they live? Were they born in the United States? If not, when and why did they come here? Where did you get your family name? Is it German? Puerto Rican? Vietnamese? Something else? If you are adopted, what is your adoptive family's story?

By searching for the answers to these questions, you can begin to discover your family's history. And if your family history is hard to trace, team up with a friend to share ideas or to learn more about that person's family history.

Where to Start

Start with what you know. In a notebook or on your family's computer, write down the full names of the relatives you know about and anything you know about them—where they lived, what they liked to do as children, any awards or honors they earned, and so on.

Next, gather some primary sources. Primary sources are the records and observations of eyewitnesses to events. They include diaries; letters; autobiographies; speeches; newspapers; birth, marriage, and death records; photographs; and ship records. The best primary resources about your family may be in family scrapbooks or files in your home or in your relatives' homes. You may also find some interesting material in libraries, archives, historical societies, and museums. These organizations often have primary sources available online.

The Next Steps

After taking notes and gathering primary sources, think about what facts and details you are missing. You can then prepare to interview your relatives to see if they can fill in these gaps. First, write down any questions that you would like to ask them about their lives. Then ask your relatives if they would mind being interviewed. Don't be upset if they say no. Understand that some people do not like to talk about their pasts.

Also, consider interviewing family friends. They can often provide interesting stories and details about your relatives. They might have photographs too.

Family Interviews

When you are ready for an interview, gather your questions, a notepad, a tape recorder or camcorder, and any other materials you might need. Consider showing your interview subjects a photograph or a timetable of important events at the start of your interview. These items can help jog the memory of your subjects and get them talking. You might also bring U.S. and world maps to an interview. Ask your subjects to label the places they have lived.

Remember that people's memories aren't always accurate. Sometimes they forget information and confuse dates. You might want to take a trip to the library or look online to check dates and other facts.

Get Organized!

When you finish your interviews and research, you are ready to organize your information. There are many ways of doing this. You can write a history of your entire family or individual biographies of your relatives. You can create a timeline going back to your earliest known ancestors. You can make a family tree—a diagram or chart that shows how people in your family are related to one another.

If you have collected a lot of photographs, consider compiling a photo album or scrapbook that tells your family history. Or if you used a camcorder to record your interviews, you might even want to make a movie.

However you put together your family history, be sure to share it! Your relatives will want to see all the information you found. You might want to create a website or blog so that other people can learn about your family. Whatever you choose to do, you'll end up with something your family will appreciate for years to come.

AFRICAN AMERICAN SNAPSHOT

African Americans are generally black Americans who trace their roots to sub-Saharan Africa (Africa south of the Sahara). U.S. society doesn't consider Americans from North Africa—north of the Sahara—to be African American.

Most African Americans are the descendants of slaves. Their families have lived in the United States for generations. But in the late 1900s and early 2000s, the number of new immigrants from Africa jumped dramatically. The chart below shows the five main African countries from which people have immigrated to the United States since 1960, the top five states in which they settled, and the years of highest immigration from each country.

COUNTRY	TOTAL POPULATION IN 2000 U.S. CENSUS	YEARS OF HIGHEST IMMIGRATION (IN DESCENDING ORDER)	FIVE TOP STATES OF RESIDENCE (IN DESCENDING ORDER)
Ethiopia	2,385,216	2006, 2008, 2007, 2005	California, Virginia, Maryland, Texas, Minnesota
South Africa	1,212,465	2005, 2001, 2002, 2004	California, New Jersey, New York, Texas, Virginia
Nigeria	164,691	2006, 2007, 2008, 2005	Texas, New York, Maryland, California, New Jersey
Cape Verde	77,103	2007, 2008, 2006, 2005	Massachusetts, Rhode Island, New York, Connecticut, California
Ghana	49,944	2006, 2007, 2008, 2005	California, Virginia, Maryland, Texas, Florida

GLOSSARY

abolish: to do away with

acoustic guitar: a guitar that does not use an electronic amplifier

Allah: the name for God in the Islamic religion

blues music: a type of slow, sad music with roots in western Africa, invented by African Americans in the South. The music is based on certain rhythms and chord progressions and was originally focused on guitar, bass, drums, and voice.

Christianity: a religion based on the life and teachings of Jesus Christ

Civil War: the U.S. war between the Confederacy, or Southern states, and the Union, or Northern states, from 1861 to 1865. African American slavery was a key issue that led to this war.

discrimination: unfair behavior toward others based on differences in race, age, gender, or other cultural factors

Islam: a religion based on the teachings of Muhammad, who was born in Saudi Arabia in about 570 A.D.

Kwanzaa: an African American holiday based on traditional African harvest festivals. The holiday was created in 1967 by scholar Ron Karenga and takes place every year from December 26 to January 1.

Muslim: a follower of Islam. Muslims believe in a God they call Allah and that Muhammad is Allah's prophet.

pidgin: a homegrown mixture of English and another language

pilgrimage: a journey to worship at a holy place

professional: a person who gets paid for doing something

segregate: to separate people by race, age, gender, or other social factors

spiritual: a type of religious folk song originated by African Americans in the South

worship: to express devotion to a divine being, often during a formal service with other worshippers

SOURCE NOTE

34–35 Vivian Chakarian, "Arthur Ashe: Tennis Champion and Civil Rights Activist," Voice of America, September 18, 2005, http://www.voanews.com/specialenglish/archive/2005-09/2005-09-18-voa1.cfm (January 19, 2010).

SELECTED BIBLIOGRAPHY

Copage, Eric V. *Kwanzaa: An African-American Celebration of Culture and Cooking*. New York: Harper Perennial, 1993.
This book is part cookbook and part exploration of the history of Kwanzaa. It includes recipes from Africa, the Caribbean, and the United States.

Educational Broadcasting Corporation. "African American World." PBS. 2005. http://www.pbs.org/wnet/aaworld (December 23, 2009).
This interactive guide to African American culture features sections on history, arts and culture, race and society, and profiles of famous African Americans.

Holloway, Joseph E., ed. *Africanisms in American Culture*. Bloomington: Indiana University Press, 1995.
This selection of academic articles examines the influence of African culture on American culture.

Maffly-Kipp, Laurie. "African American Religion, Pt. I: To the Civil War." TeacherServe from the National Humanities Center. N.d. http://nationalhumanitiescenter.org/tserve/nineteen/nkeyinfo/aareligion.htm (December 23, 2009).
This article describes the religious history of Africans in the United States up until the Civil War.

Mintz, Sidney W., and Richard Price. *The Birth of African-American Culture: An Anthropological Perspective*. Boston: Beacon Press, 1992.
Written by two anthropologists, this book explores the links between African and African American cultures.

Schomburg Center for Research in Black Culture. *Jubilee: The Emergence of African-American Culture*. Washington, DC: National Geographic, 2002.
This collection of essays by prominent voices in African American history and literature explores topics such as slavery, African American family life, religion, language, and more.

Shropshire, Kenneth L. *In Black and White: Race and Sports in America*. New York: New York University Press, 1996.
This book examines African Americans in U.S. sports.

Whitaker, Matthew C., ed. *African American Icons of Sport: Triumph, Courage, and Excellence*. Westport, CT: Greenwood Press, 2008.
This collection includes articles on the Williams sisters, Shaquille O'Neal, Magic Johnson, Muhammad Ali, the Negro Baseball Leagues, Arthur Ashe, and more.

Wills, David W., ed. "African-American Religion: A Documentary History Project." AARDOC. 2006. http://www3.amherst.edu/~aardoc (January 19, 2010).
This website provides a comprehensive history of African American religion, from the earliest encounters of Europeans and Africans along the west coast of Africa in the mid-fifteenth century to the present day.

Wolfram, Walt, and Erik Thomas. *The Development of African American English*. San Francisco: Blackwell Publishers, 2002.
This book examines the development of language by slaves and their descendants.

FURTHER READING AND WEBSITES

African American World for Kids
http://pbskids.org/aaworld/index.html
This website from PBS Kids and National Public Radio features a section where you can learn about events in African American history and then make e-cards about them.

Brill, Marlene Targ. *Marshall "Major" Taylor: World Champion Bicyclist, 1899–1901*. Minneapolis: Twenty-First Century Books, 2008.
This biography of Major Taylor, the bicycle-racing superstar of the early part of the twentieth century, tells the story of a black man competing in the white cycling world.

Greene, Meg. *Into the Land of Freedom: African American Reconstruction*. Minneapolis: Twenty-First Century Books, 2004.
The end of the Civil War and the passing of the Thirteenth Amendment ushered in an era of dramatic change known as Reconstruction. This book discusses how freed African Americans reunited with family, set up churches and schools, and voted for the first time.

HarlemLIVE
http://www.harlemlive.org
This website made by and for teens explores the organizations, events, and people of Harlem.

Kwanzaa
http://www.history.com/minisites/kwanzaa
Learn about the history, principles, and symbols of this important African American holiday.

Landau, Elaine. *Fleeing to Freedom on the Underground Railroad: The Courageous Slaves, Agents, and Conductors*. Minneapolis: Twenty-First Century Books, 2006.
This book about fugitive slaves headed for freedom tells the story of the slaves and the people who helped them. This effort grew into a secret network known as the Underground Railroad.

Manheimer, Ann. *Martin Luther King Jr: Dreaming of Equality*. Minneapolis: Twenty-First Century Books, 2005.
This books tells the story of Martin Luther King Jr. It explores his passion and commitment, which led him to become the leader of the civil rights movement.

Nabwire, Constance, and Bertha Vining Montgomery. *Cooking the West African Way*. Minneapolis: Lerner Publications Company, 2002.
This illustrated cookbook presents recipes from West African nations.

Nelson, Kadir. *We Are the Ship: The Story of Negro Baseball*. New York: Jump at the Sun/Hyperion Books for Children, 2008.
Learn about the history of African American baseball players from the 1800s and 1900s. This book, divided into nine innings, discusses the discrimination faced by players in the Negro Leagues.

Sanna, Ellyn. *American Regional Cooking Library: African American*. Bloomall, PA: Mason Crest Publishers, 2004.
Learn how to make your own fried catfish, sweet potato fries, peach cobbler, and more.

USA Today Lifeline Biographies. Minneapolis: Twenty-First Century Books, 2009–2010.
Read profiles of Barack Obama, Will Smith, and other prominent African Americans in this series.

WayBack: Stand Up for Your Rights
http://pbskids.org/wayback/civilrights/index.html
On this website you can read about African American kids who broke the race barrier at Little Rock's Central High School and take a civil rights quiz.

INDEX

Aaron, Hank, 33
Academy Awards, 25, 26
Africa, 6, 7, 17, 42, 53, 56, 63; recipe from, 64; religion and holidays from, 42, 43, 45, 47, 56
African immigrants, newest, 5, 7, 40, 47; food of, 63–65
African Methodist Episcopal (AME) Church, 44–45
Ali, Muhammad, 31–32
Angelou, Maya, 70
art and crafts, 27
Ashe, Arthur, 34–35
athlete activists, 31
athletes. *See* sports

baseball, 29, 30, 33, 39–40
basketball, 28, 29, 30, 36, 37
Berry, Chuck, 20
Berry, Halle, 25
Black Nativity, 52
blood bank, inventor of, 70
blues music, 18–19
boxing, 31–32
Br'er Rabbit tales, 10
Brown, James, 20–21
Bryant, Kobe, 28

Carver, George Washington, 5
Chamillionaire, 23
Charles, Ray, 20
Christianity, 17, 43–46, 51–52
Christmas, 51–52
civil rights movement, 5, 31, 71; religion and, 45
clothing, Muslim, 14, 47, 48, 25
cornmeal, 60
Creole cooking, 61

discrimination: racial, 5, 22, 23, 24, 31, 34–35; religious, 48–49; in sports, 28–29, 30, 31, 33
Drew, Charles, 70
DuBois, W. E. B., 10–11
Dungy, Tony, 28

Ebonics, 9
Ebony, 15
education, 7, 8, 9, 10, 44; all-black colleges, 29
Ellison, Ralph, 11

Farrakhan, Louis, 48
food, 47, 58–69; recipes, 64, 68
football, 28, 30, 38
Franklin, Aretha, 21

Gordy, Berry, 21. *See also* Motown
Gullah language, 8, 18

Handy, W. C., 19
Harlem Renaissance, 22, 24
health issues, 67, 69, 70
holidays, 50–57; Christmas, 51–52; Islamic, 57; Kwanzaa, 51, 53–56; naming ceremonies, 56–57
Hughes, Langston, 11, 52
Hurston, Zora Neale, 11

"I have a dream" speech, 12, 13
Islam, 32, 42, 43, 47–49, 63, 70; holidays of, 57; Nation of Islam, 48

Jackson, Michael, 21–22
jazz, 19
Jeter, Derek, 40, 70
juke, 18

King, Martin Luther, Jr., 12, 13, 45
Kwanzaa, 51, 53–56

languages, 6–9, 18, 53; Ebonics, 9; Gullah, 8, 18
Latifa, Queen, 71
Lee, Spike, 25
Lee-Smith, Hughie, 27
literature, 9–15, 70; oral, 8, 9–10, 12, 70

magazines, 11, 15, 32
McDaniel, Hattie, 24–25
minstrel shows, 22
Mo'Nique, 25–26
Moon, Warren, 38
Morrison, Toni, 14
Motown, 21. *See also* Gordy, Berry
movies, 21, 24–26, 71
music, 16, 17–22, 23, 71; religion and, 42, 43, 45, 46, 52; slavery and, 17–18
Muslims. *See* Islam

NAACP, 11
naming ceremonies, 56–57
Nation of Islam, 48

Obama, Barack, 5, 12, 13, 71; books by, 15
Olympics, 29, 32, 35, 36, 41

paintings, 27
Parks, Rosa, 71
poets, 15
Pope, Eddie, 40
poverty, 9, 19, 46–47, 61
Precious: Based on the Novel 'Push' by Sapphire, 25–26
president, U.S., 5, 12, 13, 15, 71

ragtime, 19
rap and hip–hop, 22, 23, 71
religion, 9, 17, 32, 42–47, 50; Christianity, 17, 43–46, 51–52; civil rights and, 45; Islam, 32, 42, 43, 47–49, 70; Nation of Islam, 48; in slavery, 42–44. *See also* holidays

Robeson, Paul, 24
Robinson, Jackie, 30, 39
rock 'n' roll, 19, 20–22
Roots, 14
Ross, Diana, and the Supremes, 21
Rudolph, Wilma, 35–36

September 11, 48, 49
sharecroppers, 18
Sidibe, Gabourey, 25
slavery, 5, 6–9, 17, 27; end of, 8; food and, 59–61, 66; music and, 17–18; religion and, 42–44, 52
slave trade, 5, 6–7
Smith, Will, 25
soccer, 40
soul food, 58, 62–63
soul music, 21–22
spirituals, 17–18
sports, 28–41, 70; all–black teams, 29; women in, 29, 35–37, 41
storytelling, 10

Taylor, Marshall, 29
tea cakes, 66–67; recipe, 68
television, 25, 71
tennis, 34–35, 36
theater, 22, 24, 52
track and field, 29, 32, 35–36

Walker, Alice, 14
wars: in Africa, 7; Civil War, 5; Vietnam, 32
Washington, Denzel, 25
Waters, Muddy, 19
Williams, Serena, 36, 37
Williams, Venus, 36, 37
Winfrey, Oprah, 25, 71
Woods, Tiger, 41
work, 9, 18, 19, 23, 39, 62
Wright, Richard, 11
writers, 10–12, 14–15, 70

PHOTO ACKNOWLEDGMENTS

The images in this book are used with the permission of: © Stefan Zaklin/epa/CORBIS, pp. 3 (top), 4; © Handout/USA TODAY, pp. 3 (second from top), 12; © Jack Gruber/USA TODAY, pp. 3 (third from top), 25; © Robert Hanashiro/USA TODAY, pp. 3 (forth from top), 28, 38, 62, 71(bottom); AP Photo/Wally Santana, pp. 3 (third from bottom), 16; © JOHN ZIOMEK/Courier-Post/USA TODAY, pp. 3 (second from bottom), 53; © Robert Deutsch/USA TODAY, pp. 3 (bottom), 61, 70 (bottom); The Granger Collection, New York, p. 6; © Herbert Orth/Time Life Pictures/Getty Images, p. 10; © Julie Schmalz/USA TODAY, p. 13; © USA TODAY, pp. 14, 20, 48, 70 (top),71 (second from top); © Transcendental Graphics/Getty Images, pp. 15, 30; © Michael Ochs Archives/Getty Images, p. 19; © Santa Fabio/USA TODAY, p. 21;© Bob Riha Jr./USA TODAY, pp. 23, 42; © George Karger/Time & Life Pictures/Getty Images, p. 24; Art © Estate of Hughie Lee-Smith/Licensed by VAGA, New York, NY/Smithsonian American Art Musuem/Art Resource, NY, p. 27; © AFP/Getty Images, p. 31; © Michael Schwarz/USA TODAY, pp. 33, 46; © Focus on Sport/Getty Images, p. 34; © Popperfoto/Getty Images, p. 35; © William West/AFP/Getty Images, p. 36; © Steven Freeman/NBAE/Getty Images, p. 37; © J. Miranda/Major League Soccer/Getty Images, p. 40; © Thomas Delay/AFP/Getty Images, p. 41; Mid-Manhattan Picture Collection /The New York Public Library, Astor, Lenox and Tilden foundations, p. 44; Michael A. Schwartz/USA TODAY, p. 46; AP Photo/Craig Lassig, p. 47; © Ariel Skelley/Blend Images/Getty Images, p. 50; © Steve Dunwell/The Image Bank/Getty Images, p. 51; © Greg Ryan/Alamy, p. 52; AP Photo/Mike Derer, p. 57; © Todd Plitt, USA TODAY, pp. 58, 71 (top); © Lew Robertson/Brand X Pictures/Getty Images, p. 60 (top); © Leigh Beisch/Getty Images, p. 60 (bottom); © ERHARDT KRAUSE/ZUMA Press, p. 65; © Inti St. Clair/Getty Images, p. 67; © Randy Faris/Corbis Premium RF/Alamy, p. 69; © Alfred Eisenstaedt/Time & Life Pictures/Getty Images, p. 70 (center);Gannett News Service, Donna Terek/The Detroit News, p. 71 (second from bottom).

Front cover: (left) © George McNish/Star Ledger/Corbis, (top right); © Mark Adams/Taxi/Getty Images; (top left) © iStockphoto.com/ John Peacock.

ABOUT THE AUTHOR

Children's and YA author Sandy Donovan has written numerous titles, including *Running for Office: A Look at Political Campaigns, Iranians in America*, and three titles in the USA TODAY Cultural Mosaic series. Donovan is a graduate of the Humphrey Institute of Public Policy at the University of Minnesota and lives in Minneapolis, Minnesota.